P9-BYS-178

The Mutation

Even the book morphs!
Flip the pages
and check it out!

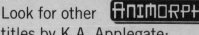

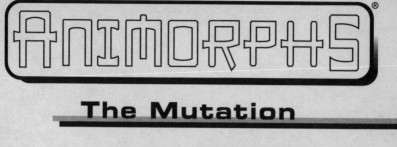

The Mutation

K.A. Applegate

AN
APPLE
PAPERBACK

SCHOLASTIC INC.
New York Toronto London Auckland Sydney
Mexico City New Delhi Hong Kong

Cover illustration by David B. Mattingly
Art Direction/Design by Karen Hudson

ISBN 0-439-10675-3

12 11 10 9 8 7 6 5 4 3 2 1   9/9 0 1 2 3 4/0

Printed in the U.S.A.
First Scholastic printing, December 1999

The author wishes to thank Erica Bobone for her help in preparing this manuscript.

For Michael and Jake

The Mutation

CHAPTER 1

A phone call at three A.M. is rarely a good thing.

When you're an Animorph, the chance of good news ever — day or night — is zero.

"Jake?"

Cassie's voice sounded shaky. Frightened.

"What's up?" I said, my own voice casual. At the same time praying that no one else in my house had picked up the phone. "Those math problems giving you a hard time?"

Cassie forced a laugh. "No. Just can't sleep again. You know, same old thing."

"Try counting sheep. I bet before you get to thirty you'll be asleep."

"Good idea. Thanks, Jake. See you."

1

Cassie hung up the phone.

I had a half hour to get from the subdivision where I live with my family to the farm Cassie shares with her parents.

Who knew when I'd be back. Forget about getting any more sleep.

I stripped off my pajamas in the dark.

Opened my window wide.

Gave one last glance over my shoulder at the closed door of my bedroom. No lights on in the hallway. Good.

Then I looked out at the star-studded night and concentrated on the image of a bird.

Peregrine falcon.

I began to shrink. From a normal human kid, maybe a bit larger than average, to a one-foot-high human kid.

I heard my internal organs changing. A squirmy sound, like a rumbling stomach, a sound you feel more than hear.

It's a big change going from human to bird. Nothing ends up where it starts out. You go from a system designed to eat a bit of this and a bit of that, all well-chewed, to a system designed to swallow whole mice and poop out the bones and fur.

My own bones, my big, solid human bones shrank and hollowed out. Finger bones relatively longer, leg bones shorter, breast bone huge.

2

My skin tightened over the new skeleton. Flesh melted, ran together, like hot wax. I had wings instead of arms. Skinny legs and dangerous talons.

Gray-and-white feather patterns etched themselves onto my still semisoft skin, then raised into three dimensions.

Fleshy human nose and mouth blurred, ran together, then extended out to become a hard beak. My eyes became smaller in absolute terms, but much larger in relative terms.

I was ready.

I hopped onto my desk. From there, onto the windowsill. And then I flew.

My name is Jake.

We're not supposed to like it, this power we have. We being me, my best bud Marco, my cousin Rachel, Cassie and Tobias and Ax. We're not supposed to like it, but mostly I do. This power to morph. To touch an animal and by doing so acquire its DNA. To become that animal at will.

In the wrong hands this incredible power can be seriously abused. In our own fumbling, uncertain human hands this power is both a privilege and a curse.

We learned the truth about morphing the hard way, back in the beginning. Back when the five of us — Ax hadn't joined the team yet — witnessed

3

an Andalite spaceship land in an abandoned construction site. And a dying alien emerge.

A pale blue deerlike creature with the torso of a muscular man. Two huge almond-shaped eyes in his face. Two more eyes on stalks that grew out of the top of his head and swiveled to look behind, right and left.

No mouth. But what a tail! Long and strong. With a sharp, curved blade on the end. Deadly. Lightning fast.

A warrior prince named Elfangor.

With the last of his strength Elfangor told us of the galaxywide invasion of a parasitic species called Yeerks. Gray slugs that insinuate themselves into the brains of sentient creatures.

That crawl through the ear canal and wrap themselves in and around the brain.

Spread and seep into every crevice.

Read and laugh at every painful memory and embarrassing desire you've ever had. Like striking out in your first Little League game. Like wanting so badly for the prettiest girl in class to smile at you.

You are the slave of this thing. The real you rages then eventually cowers somewhere in the back of your skull.

Watching as the Yeerk uses you, controls you, turns you into yet another instrument of Yeerk domination.

4

The Yeerks are everywhere.

Your parents. Your lab partner. The lead singer in your favorite band. Your regular garbage man.

Any of these people might have a Yeerk in their head. Might be what we call a human-Controller.

My brother Tom is one. His bedroom is two doors down from mine. Marco's mother is a Controller. We don't know where she is.

Our vice principal, Chapman, is one. How many more? We don't know. More. Always more.

We are not winning this war. We're delaying the final defeat. No more than that. Maybe not as much as that.

For some reason I'm the leader of this little band of warriors. I'm still not sure how it happened but I've stopped fighting the fact.

Sometimes I'm secretly proud when Aximili-Esgarrouth-Isthill, the Andalite cadet who joined us not long after we encountered his older brother Elfangor, calls me "Prince" Jake.

Mostly embarrassed, but there are times when it feels okay.

I'm proud when we're winning. When we're "kicking Yeerk butt" as Rachel would say. I'm also proud when we don't win but have done the best we could. Acted with courage and honor.

Most of the time I'm also terrified.

Like when I heard Cassie's trembling voice on the other end of the line.

5

I flew to the barn that houses the Wildlife Rehabilitation Center Cassie's dad operates.

I landed out back and when I was sure it was safe, began to demorph.

Voices. From inside the barn. Low and worried.

Cassie . . . and Hork-Bajir.

CHAPTER 2

"This is a terrible thing he has done." Toby Hamee's voice was grave.

I didn't answer. I didn't understand, yet.

Cassie knelt by the side of a Hork-Bajir. He could no longer speak. He could barely breathe. He was laid out on the stainless steel table Cassie's dad uses to perform operations.

He was seven feet tall. Too tall to fit easily on the table. His legs hung off. His bladed arms hung off.

He was clearly Hork-Bajir. Just as clearly he was something else, as well.

The barn is a dark place even in the daytime. But now it was gloom inside of gloom. There were rows and shelves of caged, sick, convalescing an-

7

imals. Mostly quiet. The occasional mutter or growl or chirp.

"Cassie?"

She turned to look up at me. Her eyes were dull with agony.

"He can't get enough air," she said. "His pulse is weak."

"Make fish! He try to make fish-people!" Jara Hamee cried.

I turned to Toby. A seer of her people. More intelligent and articulate than her fellow Hork-Bajir, including her father, Jara.

"Who?"

"Visser Three," Toby said. "Who else?"

"What happened?"

"This is Hahn Tunad. He was not a free Hork-Bajir. Not one of our colony. Now Hahn is free of the Yeerks but he is dying for it." Toby paused before going on. "Hahn and forty-nine other Hork-Bajir were the subjects of an experiment. I have come to understand from Hahn that the visser is obsessed with rediscovering the Pemalite ship. He is very angry that his last attempt was foiled by the being called the Drode. And by the so-called Andalite bandits."

"Okay," I said, watching Cassie wipe a cool cloth over Hahn's bladed forehead. "Go on."

"The visser attempted to produce an amphibious creature. To aid in this deep-sea mis-

8

sion. He failed. When he realized the fifty test subjects were useless to him, he ordered their Yeerks to abandon the now-useless host bodies. They were to be fed to the Taxxons. We found Hahn . . . the others were already dead."

Toby nodded toward her distraught father. "They were friends. Long ago."

I tried to slow my racing heart. To breathe deeply. To keep from vomiting.

I knelt by Cassie.

She pointed to Hahn's left shoulder. Just below the blade was — a gill. I'd already seen it. I'd seen the webs between the Hork-Bajir talons and fingers, too.

"Jake, the visser just grafted these gills onto the body," Cassie whispered. "It's as if he and his medical team had no idea of Hork-Bajir physiology. It's all wrong. Totally botched!"

"Feet! Feet!" Jara, more agitated than I'd ever seen him, pointed to Hahn's feet.

"Jake, he can't breathe. I don't know what they did inside, to his lungs . . ."

I grabbed the oxygen mask from the ground where Cassie had dropped it in defeat. Yanked the oxygen tank closer to the makeshift bed of hay bales.

"Jake! You can't . . . it's too late!"

Pushing past Cassie I held the mask to Hahn's mouth. Opened the valve on the tank.

9

"Jake, you're not doing him any good. He's in pain. No one can help him."

She gently pulled the mask away.

From behind me I was dimly aware of Toby's voice.

"Hahn was able to tell us of a powerful new seagoing vessel the visser has built specifically for the purpose of locating the Pemalite ship. It is known as the Sea Blade."

A horrible gurgling rose from Hahn's throat.

"Cassie! Something's caught in his throat!"

"A valve of some sort," she said. "It's malfunctioning. I tried to open it. Tried to keep it from closing further. I couldn't."

Jara stepped forward and gracefully took one of Hahn's hands. "Hahn not die!" he pleaded. "Hahn come with Toby and Jara and be free!"

"No, Father. It is time for Hahn to go Beyond. Our friends, Tobias and the others, will help us destroy the evil that is Visser Three. Help us avenge Hahn's death."

With a terrible sob, Jara knelt and gently laid his bladed head on Hahn's body.

And then there was one less sound in the barn. One less creature breathing.

I moved away. Jara needed privacy. I turned to look up at the window in the rafters. Tobias's favorite passage into and out of the barn.

The sky was beginning to lighten. Dawn was approaching.

A new day. A day Hahn and the other mutated Hork-Bajir would never see.

"Jake?"

I looked back to Cassie. Opened my arms. She came to me and we held each other.

We held each other until Toby and Jara had wrapped Hahn's body in blankets and taken him into the sunrise.

CHAPTER 3

It was after school the next day and we were in Cassie's barn. Where only hours earlier a mutated Hork-Bajir lay dying.

"We have to go after the Sea Blade, period," Rachel said angrily. "We definitely can't let the Yeerks get hold of the Pemalite ship. Or Pemalite technology."

"A plan would be nice," Marco said.

<We don't know enough to make any plans,> Tobias argued from his usual perch and lookout in the rafters.

Tobias is a *nothlit*. Someone who stayed in morph for longer than the two hour limit. Now he's a red-tailed hawk first, all other creatures second.

12

Rachel gives him a hard time about staying hawk and not going back to being a regular human boy twenty-four seven. But the explanation is there if you want to see it. If Tobias gives up his ability to morph by trapping himself in human form, he's out of the fight. And he can't walk away from this war. He can't — or won't — abandon us.

Tobias is Elfangor's son. Long story. Weird story.

<Yes, though we can make use of the additional information we received from Toby's spies this morning,> Ax pointed out.

Right after dawn I'd sent Ax and Tobias to the secret community the free Hork-Bajir had established. Their information was sketchy. Hork-Bajir, with the exception of Toby, are not the brightest species around. It's a little like asking a four-year-old to describe a movie.

But we'd also tapped into the Chee network. The Chee are a whole different story. Androids are very good at description. The Chee didn't know much, but what they knew was different. They had seen different pieces of the puzzle.

"What *do* we know? That's the question," Marco said.

I nodded at Ax. "Ax-man? Give us a run-down."

13

<We know very little. We can extrapolate and guess a bit more,> Ax said.

I smiled. "So include the guesses and the extrapolation."

<The Sea Blade is a new type of vessel. It can travel in the air and in the water. Most spacecraft can travel under water for a short distance, and with limited effect. But in order for the Yeerks to travel to Earth's deepest oceans they would need something radically different,> Ax said. <It seems likely that both in the air, and in the water, this vessel will be able to cloak itself from normal human sensors.>

"It would have to," Marco interjected. "Too many subs out there in the deep, blue sea. There are still sensors all over the ocean floor from the Cold War."

<Exactly,> Ax agreed.

"Echolocation?" Cassie suggested.

"Echolocation is a lot like what they call 'active sonar,'" Marco said. "You bounce sound waves off an object and listen to the echoes. But subs don't use active sonar, usually, because if you're 'pinging' someone with active sonar, they can hear you. Subs usually stick with passive listening."

"Marco, are you just pulling all this out of the air? How do you know all this?" Rachel demanded.

14

"Tom Clancy."

I nodded. "Tom Clancy. *The Hunt for Red October.*"

"You should read something besides *Glamour,* Rachel."

"So would echolocation work, or not?" Cassie demanded.

We all looked at Ax. <Maybe. Maybe not. But it is all we have to work with.>

Cassie chewed her lip. "I'm thinking giant squid, if we're going real deep. Or dolphins or whales," Cassie said.

<The Chee have revealed the location of the Pemalite ship to us. It is deep, but not terribly deep. However, it is in an area designated as a Navy firing range. There are large numbers of exploded . . . and unexploded . . . weapons. Humans would be unlikely to frequent the area.>

Tobias said, <Why don't the Chee just get to the Pemalite ship and move it before the Yeerks show up?>

"The Yeerks will just keep looking," I said. "The Chee can't get into a game of hide-and-seek. Sooner or later they'd lose. And if the Pemalite ship is moving it's easier to detect."

"We have to sink the Sea Blade," Cassie said quietly. "We have to sink it, destroy it. Make them regret ever thinking about invading the ocean."

15

I shot her a look. It wasn't like Cassie to be bloodthirsty.

She met my gaze, unflinching. "What they did to the Hork-Bajir was evil," she said. "Over the line. *Way* over the line. We need to teach them a lesson."

I nodded. I understood her feelings. But this mission couldn't be about feelings.

Marco said what I was thinking. "Hey, we don't teach lessons. And we don't do revenge. Besides, everything the Yeerks do is over the line. We stop them. That's what we do."

Cassie looked unconvinced. Rachel was smirking in cocky agreement with Cassie. Rachel liked the idea of delivering a harsh lesson. I expected that from Rachel. But from Cassie it worried me.

There were problems here for me, as the leader of this bunch of tired, stressed-out misfits. Tobias hated going into the water. Marco wasn't convinced it was necessary. Cassie was taking it all personally.

Rachel and Ax were their usual selves. I sighed. Fairly typical: At any given point, on any given mission, maybe half the team was going to be difficult in one way or another. Including me, of course. Maybe especially me.

"Echolocation," Cassie mused. "We've all got dolphin morphs."

16

<Rachel and I have sperm whale morphs,> Tobias reminded us.

"And we all do giant squid," Rachel said.

"Not sure we want to deal with those guys again," Marco mumbled. "Creepy."

"Whales are good. We need a morph we can control. Something intelligent. That can dive deep and do some serious damage to the Sea Blade," I said. "But let's face it. The chances of another sperm whale beaching itself just for the rest of us to acquire are pretty slim."

"Of course!" Cassie snapped her fingers. "There's an orca — a killer whale — at The Gardens' SeaTown. They're calling him Swoosh."

"Swoosh?" Marco repeated incredulously. "Who names these animals?"

Cassie looked embarrassed. "Nike. They sponsored the exhibit. So they got to name the whale."

"Okay," I said. "We need to get going. A) I contact the Chee and alert them to be ready to take our places. B) we carry out round-the-clock surveillance on the vicinity of the Yeerk pool. Try and spot any sign of this Sea Blade launching. C) we acquire the killer whale."

"Easy," Marco mocked. "ABC. Just don't mention, D) we chase a super sub into the ocean, and E) try to destroy it before, F) they reach an alien

17

spacecraft in the middle of, G) a bunch of unexploded bombs and shells that may get set off when the Yeerks try to, H) fry us with their Dracon beams."

Rachel laughed and gave Marco a playful shove. "You're always so negative. Look on the bright side: Maybe the unexploded shells will, I) blow up the Yeerks, not us."

Cassie wasn't joining in the graveyard humor. "Fifty Hork-Bajir subjected to horrible medical experiments," she said. "*That's* what this is about."

CHAPTER 4

<We've got a math test on Friday, Big Jake.>

<Since when are you so concerned about school?> I asked. It didn't matter. We were just making conversation. Killing the boring two hours of our shift.

I was at about fifty feet. Marco was another twenty-five feet or so higher, and two or three blocks to the east. We were two birds of prey, a falcon and an osprey, riding the thermals, floating on the cushions of warm air.

<Since the math teacher married my dad. It's a crime, that's what it is. Had to be math. Couldn't have been some subject I can fake my way through. No. Has to be math. The answer is either the square root of pi or it isn't, dude, there's

19

no bull factor. I can't say, "Well, I felt what the writer really meant was . . .">

<The Chee who plays you will take the test.>

<Exactly. And he'll get the grade I would have gotten. I don't want the grade I would have gotten. I want an A. But not a perfect A. A just barely there, A. She'd buy that. Maybe.>

<You're assuming you won't be there for the test,> I said. <Way things are going . . . I mean, we got nothing.>

Marco and I had been on patrol for an hour and a half. Our third day of floating in bird-of-prey morph, high above the area that concealed the Yeerk pool.

The Yeerk pool is a huge, underground complex. A central dome bigger than a football stadium, plus tunnels and satellite areas. It stretches beneath part of the mall, and all the way over to the school, with a bunch of fast-food restaurants and car lots and streets in between.

We knew the Sea Blade was in the Yeerk pool complex. Which meant, sooner or later, that it would emerge. How? When? Where? We didn't have a clue. And I was awfully sick and tired of getting a peregrine falcon's up close and incredibly personal view of roofs and trash and people in cars.

In a few minutes Ax and Tobias would show up so Marco and I could demorph, remorph, and

20

fly home. I was counting the minutes. I wanted to veg out and watch some TV. With weak human eyes.

Let's see. What night was it? Was there anything on? I couldn't even remember what day of the — <Marco! I'm seeing something!>

<You mean that girl in the bathing suit driving that Mazda?>

<The vacant lot next to the Walgreen's, man!>

I glanced up and saw Marco wheel around to come closer. I focused back on the empty lot. There was a fence around it. A fairly new chain-link fence armed with razor wire at the top.

I cursed my own stupidity. Why hadn't I thought about that? Who would protect an empty lot with a new fence? It made no sense. Unless the lot wasn't so empty.

<Shimmering? Is that what you mean?> Marco asked.

<It's a hologram,> I yelled. <The sides are maintaining, but the top is breaking up.>

It was the kind of thing that would have seemed so weird to me a while back. Before. Back when I lived a normal life. Now Marco yelled <hologram!> and I thought, *Well, duh. Of course it's a hologram.*

The hologram showed the field. The empty field. Seen from any angle you'd see an empty, scruffy-looking rectangle of weeds and bare, tan

21

dirt, rusty soda cans, and shredded McDonald's trash.

But looking straight down from above, something else began to appear.

Enormous! Two scimitar-shaped wings. A sleek body, built for speed. Not the elongated teardrop shape of a human sub. More like a Yeerk Blade ship, but with pustulelike pods extruding here and there around the hull.

It was blacker than black. Like something carved out of anthracite. In the brief moments it was visible it seemed to drain the light from the sky. To absorb all color into its endless black depths.

It rested on a rising platform. Like one of those hydraulic car lifts at a gas station. It was being lifted up through the roof of the Yeerk pool, up through an oblong tunnel cut through packed dirt and rock.

And then it began to shimmer and fade, just as the hologram had done. A hum grew into a low roar that even passersby would have heard, except that the only traffic was cars rushing past.

<It's going, man!>

<Yeah. It'll head for the water.>

<I'm on it,> I said.

Marco didn't argue. Ospreys are fast. Peregrines are faster.

<Get the others. Ax and Tobias should be here

22

soon, you'll probably pass them. Send them after me. You get Rachel and Cassie.>

I took off, heading for the sea. I'd need all the head start I could get.

<How are we going to find you?> Marco said, his voice tense. He was already banking away toward home.

<I don't know. Just get to the ocean as fast as you can. I'll . . . >

SWOOOOZZSH!

Straight up! The Sea Blade lifted up off the ground, rose like it was a Styrofoam stage prop being lifted by cables and strings. And all the while it was fading. It was an outline. A watercolor in faded colors.

And then it was gone! Cloaked, invisible to the naked human eye.

But not entirely hidden from the keen eyesight of the falcon. I couldn't see the ship itself. But I could make out a disturbance of the air.

Like the waves rising off hot concrete on a brutally hot day. A caloric wave or something. And then the shimmering began to move off.

I was already moving at full speed.

<Jake! Remember. Less than a half hour in this morph!>

No time to answer. I strained to gain a lead. But then it blew past, swirling me around, tumbling me through the air. I righted myself and fol-

23

lowed in the wake of the Sea Blade. Followed the blasts of hot air being expelled by the engines. Followed the occasional shimmering waves of air. The brief glances of — something.

I flapped harder. Faster. Still I was falling behind. We had calculated that a seaborne craft wouldn't be very fast through the air. It wasn't. But it was fast enough.

Already I was fading. Stupid! I should have gotten more altitude. I should have stayed as high up as I could be. How many times had Tobias told me: Altitude equals speed. I could have been using gravity to speed me. Instead gravity was my enemy.

A falcon struggling through the cool evening air was no match for the Sea Blade. The engines would not tire.

But as long as I could keep it in sight . . .

It traveled in a straight line. No tricks. No evasions. It flew straight for the beach. Suddenly it was over the sand and dunes. I was still flying hard and fast and way too low over beach bungalows and cheap motels.

I wasn't going to make it. I was exhausted. My muscles screamed in pain.

How many minutes did I have left in morph? I didn't know. Almost didn't care.

I had to keep the Sea Blade in sight. Had to

24

see which way it went once it went in. Had to at least know the general direction.

Then . . . where was the heat? Had I lost the trail? Had the Sea Blade turned away at the last minute?

No. It was powering down its air-breathing engines. Preparing to submerge. So close to shore?

The ship suddenly stopped. The shimmering wave was all in one place. No longer moving. The ship was still cloaked, invisible, as it hovered over the evening ocean.

Hit the water! I prayed.

I was minutes from being a falcon forever. It might already be too late.

For a split second a vague outline of the dark ship was visible on the ocean's surface. And then it was gone.

Exhausted, I fell to the icy water and concentrated.

And began to demorph.

Morphing is never pretty. And when you're exhausted and freezing and wet, it's seriously less than fun. Strange sounds. Disturbing sensations. Not pain exactly — but not pleasure either. You know things are happening to your body that would not happen in the normal world. That should not happen.

The demorph was fast. The falcon's natural

25

buoyancy was suddenly replaced by my very human mass. Twenty, thirty, forty pounds of torso, legs and arms.

Still growing!

I slipped under the water. Kicked back to the surface. Choked and spluttered and breathed.

I was Jake. But not for long.

CHAPTER 5

The contours of my body stretched! Shot out in every direction — up, down, forward and back, right and left.

My forehead poured out in front of me like gravel from a dump truck. My eyes migrated to the sides of my head. My ears were swallowed up in blubber.

Couldn't breathe! For a moment my throat closed. Then I felt cool, clean air again. Sucked in through the blowhole in the back of my neck.

My legs twisted around each other like a fat stick of raspberry licorice. A twenty-five-foot-long stick of licorice!

Just behind my blowhole a dorsal fin grew out of my spine and shot six and a half feet into the

27

air. An enormous jet-black triangle, taller than my human self.

My belly was a vast expanse of smooth white. My back was as black as a wet tire. My mouth filled with teeth the size of a hammer's claw head.

I was sure I was going to fill the entire ocean before the morph was complete. For a panicked second my human brain wondered how something this big could float.

And then I felt the stirrings of the orca's mind. Instincts were activated. Senses alerted brain centers.

Threats? No. There were no threats. Threats could not exist. They were an impossibility. What could challenge my power?

But prey? Ah, yes, prey could exist. Anything in the vast, endless, unmeasured ocean could be my prey. Anything bathed in seawater was my meat.

I was bigger, faster, smarter, more dangerous than anything in the ocean. I was deadly, but not with the random, malevolent violence of the shark. I could plan. I could cooperate. I could think.

In my mind were the templates, like schematics drawn with echo images. I saw the patterns of a pod of orcas moving together, communicating, working together to snare the swift sea lions, to shove the seals off their ice floes, to leap clear up onto the beach to drag a walrus to its doom.

I saw all this, I the human. And I felt the shock of seeing the familiar in a strange place. Wolves work together, like the orcas. But the closest analogy to orca behavior was found much closer to home, among my own species.

There was something very human about the killer whale's mind. Individualized, yet capable of becoming a part of a group. Capable, unlike so many creatures, of remembering a past, imagining a future.

I sensed, deep within the orca mind, the images of my prey. The rubbery, swift-moving penguins and sea otters and sea lions and walruses. Even the dolphins. And, when they grew weak, when they had lost their force and their speed, the great whales themselves.

I have inhabited many animal minds. The prey animals want to stay alive, to hide, to run, to find food, to find mates. The predators look for prey, for the weak and vulnerable. They mark and defend territories. They seek mates.

Always they are simple, compared to humans. Almost always their minds are black and white, coded with simple behaviors for simple situations.

In only a few have I encountered that strange mutation: intelligence. The capacity to see be-

29

yond fight or flee, yes or no, run or stand, kill or be killed. Only a very few species can think "If . . . then?"

The orca was one. As smart as a dolphin. As smart as a chimpanzee. It occupied that highest, most narrow rung, just below Homo sapiens.

I had encountered intelligence in a morph before. But there was something new here. New for me, at least. The orca was aware. Of me. Of something, someone directing its behavior.

It knew, in some incomplete, simplistic way, that it was being controlled.

<Let's go, big boy,> I said.

No answer from the orca, of course. But that cool, appraising intelligence, though it was devoid of memory of learning, empty of all knowledge except the knowledge encoded as instinct, that intelligence watched me.

I felt a shiver of fear. Ludicrous, of course. I was the orca, the orca could not hurt me. And yet, I felt the fear of any prey animal who finds himself under the gaze of the killer whale.

I had a mission. I fired an echolocating burst of clicks.

And suddenly there was a picture in my brain. Almost like an X ray. More like an Etch-A-Sketch drawing.

Lines and contours representing the underwater world around me. The ocean floor, smooth, sloping away. A school of fish, too small to interest me.

Then the picture was gone.

I clicked again and it was back. But now the picture included the Sea Blade.

Beneath me and further out to sea. Motionless. Almost as if it were waiting for me.

I filled my massive lungs and dove. Deeper. Deeper.

I clicked again.

The Sea Blade had to know I was here. Its sensors would have heard the echolocating clicks. Its version of sonar would have painted me. And, unlike any human crew, the Yeerks knew enough to pay attention to strange animals.

I could go after the Sea Blade myself. It was no more than a quarter mile away. But I doubted I could do much damage to the ship by myself. Let alone destroy it. If Marco and the others didn't catch up, though, I'd have no choice.

We had no plan beyond trying to keep up with the ship, try and damage it. The hardest part had seemed to be merely keeping up. But the Sea Blade just sat there. Sat, unmoving, almost silent.

How long till the others could catch up?

I surfaced for a breath. And then I saw a swift shadow moving across the water. I rolled onto my

31

side and looked up at the sky. There was a plane, a four-engine prop plane flying low, parallel to the beach. Flat gray. A military plane.

As I watched, a cylinder slid out of the back of the plane and parachuted into the sea. Seconds later I heard the splash. And then a loud pinging.

Of course! This was the Sea Blade's maiden voyage. The Yeerks were testing their new toy. The plane was a navy submarine surveillance plane dropping sonar buoys and relaying what they found down to the commander of the Sea Blade.

Depressing to realize that the Yeerks could control a navy plane. But it had worked out well for me. The test had delayed the Sea Blade.

I submerged and fired another round of echo-locating clicks.

I saw the outline of the Sea Blade. Clear and unmistakable. I fired another round, looking for . . .

Wait! Something wrong. A whale?

The Sea Blade was gone, and in its place the Etch-A-Sketch diagram of a large whale. It was huge. A humpback. Maybe even a blue whale. Precisely where the Sea Blade should have been.

What was going on?

A low hum. The sound of engines. The ship was moving away. But then, as I listened intently the engine sound became the slow whoosh,

whoosh, whoosh of a whale's flukes, driving the beast through the sea.

Then . . . behind me!

Something big, fast! More than one.

Something my orca brain recognized at once: a pod of killer whales.

<Hey, Shamu! It's me.>

Marco.

<Is everyone here?> I said.

<Yeah. Can't believe we found you.>

<Where's the Sea Blade?> Rachel asked.

<If you echolocate you'll sense a large whale moving away from us. You'll hear it, too. That, boys and girls, is the visser's new ship.>

<Yes, that would be sensible,> Ax said. <They not only hide, they create a false picture for anyone who does happen to notice them. They have adjusted the energy absorption field to reflect the picture of a whale. Generating the sound signature is easy, of course.>

<Perfect time for a surprise attack,> Rachel said. <We're like serious tonnage of battering ram here. And they're probably feeling pretty cocky.>

<More tonnage on the way. Look who's joined us,> Tobias said.

Two orcas. Not humans in morph. The real thing.

I laughed. <I appreciate their support but I don't want them getting killed for our sake.>

33

So far we were easily keeping pace with the Sea Blade. But sooner or later it would accelerate. Rachel was right. Now was as good a time as any.

<Okay, we go for the stern. What seems to be the tail in your echolocation picture. Tobias, Rachel, Marco go left. Cassie and Ax with me.>

We spread wide, seemingly a pod of orca going in two separate directions. We surfaced, Cassie, Ax, and me. We breathed deeply.

<Let's go,> I said.

It sounded so matter-of-fact. I'd begun to get used to giving orders. Probably not a good thing.

We submerged and suddenly veered for the Sea Blade. Six whales hopefully hitting the engines. That had to hurt. Had to shake something loose. Had to bust a seam and spring a few leaks.

Full power into our flukes, full speed, all that mass, had to hurt, had to do damage.

Had to.

A thousand yards. Five hundred yards.

Only two hundred yards!

I fired a burst of clicks. The Sea Blade/whale was different. Picture different. Like . . .

<It's turning!>

<He sees us!>

The sub was coming straight for us. And it had dropped all pretense of moving at whale speed. The sub was coming for us at a sudden and accelerating fifty knots.

34

CHAPTER 6

TSEEEWWW!

Dracon beam!

A horrible shrieking! An inhuman scream of pain, silenced too abruptly.

I fired clicks. Weird, impossible picture. Not six orca. Not eight. Nine.

Nine.

What?

<Oh, God!> I cried.

One of the orcas had been split lengthwise. There were two echo pictures where there should have been one.

Sliced in half! Like a loaf of Italian bread cut open to make a sandwich.

The two enormous halves of the whale began

35

to sink toward the ocean floor. The water darkened, thickened with blood.

Engulfed us! Billowed out from the torn halves of the massive creature.

<Who was hit?> I cried.

<Demorph!> Tobias yelled.

<It's not me!> Cassie answered. <Ax! Marco!>

<I am unharmed,> Ax answered.

<I'm mentally destroyed. Tell me that didn't happen.> Marco.

Relief. One of the real orca. Simple, dumb luck.

Fear. One more shot and next time . . . No chance even to avoid the beam.

No time to be afraid. Act! Do something, Jake!

<Prince Jake!>

TSEEEWWW!! TSEEEWWW!

Another yellow beam lanced the murk, missing me by millimeters.

<Jake! You've been hit!>

Impossible! I hadn't felt . . .

Another billowing red cloud surrounded me.

And then I felt the pain. I clicked and saw a piece of the whale's body, my body, spiraling down, down. The top three feet of my dorsal fin! Shaved off.

Clickclickclickclick.

36

A different angle. I needed eyes not clicks! I needed to see!

No. No, the orca chased down sea lions with its senses. It was enough. Calm down. Get a gr —

TSEEEEEW!

The Sea Blade moved again. It was over us now, a dark cloud raining killer beams.

TSEEEWW! TSEEEWWW!

<Prince Jake, you are losing too much blood! You must swim out of range and — >

TSEEEWWW!

Another foot-long slice of me was gone!

Blood. More blood.

What should I do?

<What . . . >

I was confused. Couldn't think straight.

Thunk! Thunk!

Two of us slammed into the sub. And for a moment the sub was visible to my blurred eyes. I saw the black wings, the engines, the blister pods.

The firing stopped.

<Good hit, Rachel.> Marco. His voice was far away.

And from an even greater distance, Ax. <A very impressive dent, Tobias.>

<Jake! You have to demorph! We have to get to the surface!>

I clicked weakly.

Was vaguely aware of a huge black-and-white body beneath mine, nudging.

Cassie?

<NOW Jake!>

TSEEEWWW! TSEEEWWW!

Deadly Dracon beams tore past us. I didn't care.

Cassie lifted me ten, twenty, thirty feet. Then was replaced by Ax.

<Prince Jake, you must start your demorph immediately.>

My shredded body rose. Slowly. Too slowly.

Another twenty, fifty, one hundred feet.

More than ten stories of water!

Cassie spoke. <Jake, listen. Try to morph your upper body last. If your lungs go human at this depth you'll die.>

<Cassie is correct. You must avoid decompression sickness. Start your demorph from your lower body.>

Yes. Must avoid . . .

Impossible! I wasn't Cassie. I didn't have the skill, the talent.

<I'll get you through this,> Cassie said. <You have to hold two pictures in your head. See your legs. See the whale's head.>

I concentrated. Willed myself to change.

I am Jake. Human. Human.

38

Then it began.

Eight tons of killer whale began sucking in on itself. My giant girth contracted.

I thought of feet. Legs. And felt my damaged tail go human. Become human feet, legs and —

A torso!

No! Not yet!

<Form the pictures in your mind, Jake,> Cassie said, her thought-speak voice superhumanly calm.

Still so deep! So far from the blessed surface. Fifty feet. Forty-five feet . . .

Human lungs bursting. Straining!

<See the pictures and hold on to them. Add details, see the slick black and white, see your own flesh, the little hairs, everything. The detail will hold the picture.>

The pain — it would kill me!

I felt Ax's orca body leave and once again, Cassie beneath me. Lifting the bizarre half-morphed body.

Up. Up.

Only seconds of life left . . .

<Just a few more yards, Jake.>

But I couldn't.

I was fully human. Desperately struggling for breath!

Flailing ridiculously on the back of a killer whale.

39

I couldn't . . .

Cassie's voice. Desperate now.

<Jake! Roll over onto your belly. You're just back from my blowhole. I'm going to let my air out slowly for you to take in. Listen to me, Jake. It's your only chance!>

CHAPTER 7

I woke from a gray dream.

Sprawled on the back of a killer whale.

Breathing air from its blowhole.

Carefully, weakly sucking a small mouthful of air at a time.

But this was no dream. This was my nightmarelike reality.

We breached.

Cassie blew out the last of her air along with a froth of seawater.

I started to slide off her slippery back. Grabbed onto her dorsal fin. Coughed and retched and spit out the water that had collected in my lungs.

41

<Jake?>

"I'm okay. I'm okay. I'm going to morph back to orca. You get back to the fight."

<Take a minute. Rest,> Cassie said. <Please.>

I shook my head.

"Impossible. Tell everyone to take them in the belly. Hear me? From beneath! Now go!"

I rolled off Cassie's great curved back and treaded water in the calm sea.

I watched as she descended. As she dove back into the thick of the battle. And I wondered for about two seconds if I were doing the right thing.

Then I looked up at the darkening sky and thought: killer whale.

And within minutes I became an orca for the second time that night. Eight tons and twenty feet of oceangoing, deep-diving mammal.

Below me I heard a panic of thought-speak. The confused, agitated babble you hear in old recordings of fighter planes in dogfights.

I dove and clicked. And saw the Sea Blade. Saw my friends diving beneath it.

Whoever was driving the Sea Blade knew who and what we were. He was diving, too. It was a race to the bottom. And by now we were far out to sea and the bottom was a mile below us.

TSEEEWWW! TSEEEWWW!

What had been random artillery practice was now a determined plan to eliminate the Andalite bandits.

TSEEEWWW!

Ax! His dorsal fin had been lanced clean off. There was a chunk missing from his side, like a fishmonger had sliced out a fillet.

I felt something brush my side. A floating mass of black-skinned blubber. Whose? Watched as what seemed like gallons of blood poured from the ten-foot wound.

<Ax! Get to the surface!>

<No, Prince Jake. Forgive me for disobeying your orders. I will stay as long as I am able to be of service.>

<Don't do something stupid, Ax,> I commanded. <Get out when you have to. That's an order.>

<Jake, we can't get another clear shot!> Cassie cried. <The ship's too fast. We can't get under him!>

<Yeah and this underwater Dracon beam thing is a slight prob . . . !>

TSEEEWWW!

<Aaaahhh! Aaaahhh!> Marco screamed.

TSEEEWWW!

Beneath us!

43

And now, slowly, in shimmers and fades, the ship appeared. The cloaking devices were turned off and we could see it clearly. Or as clearly as the whale's eyes could see through dark water.

It was a velvety black mass. Like some huge, dark predator animal. Hunkering down, ready to pounce. Dracon beams poised.

Why had it appeared?

No time to wonder. No choice. If we turned and ran we'd be cut up one by one. My plan was a disaster. Foolish. I'd led us all into a trap.

No time for regrets. Better to do down fighting than to sit around and wait for death.

<Okay,> I said grimly. <We'll give them what they want. All of us. We hit at the same time. Top speed.>

Marco said an extremely rude word. I couldn't blame him.

<It's what we came for,> Rachel said.

<On the count of three,> I ordered. <One. Two. Three!>

<AAAHHH!>

We dove!

Six big orca at top speed!

Like a rushing, runaway train we powered down on the Sea Blade! Until none of us could have stopped if we'd tried.

TSEEEWWW!

44

<Aaahhhh!>

TSEEEWWW!

Staggering pain. No time. Move! Keep moving! Twenty feet. Ten. Inches.

B-B-BOOOOMMMM!

We hit!

Pain seared through my head.

I clicked and saw five mammoth whale bodies rolling away and off the ship, stunned.

I rolled away. Couldn't see for a moment. My own blood clouded the water. Where was I? Where was the air?

Then the blood cleared. I could see the Sea Blade, improbably above me. No, I was turned around. And the ship was on its side.

The tail section of the Sea Blade was a mangled mess. The ship listed badly to the left. Black liquid poured from its fuselage.

<We did it!> Cassie cried. <We destroyed the Sea — !>

TSEEEWWW! TSEEEWWW! TSEEEWWW!

Yellow Dracon beams shot crazily out of the torn-up vessel! As if the ship itself was furious. Wounded and out of control.

TSEEEWWW! TSEEEWWW! TSEEEWWW!

<UGGGHHH!>

<AAAGGGHHH!>

A hideous pain in my side!

45

I clicked and saw an orca, belly sliced open. Guts spilling into the dark water.

Another orca, both flippers gone!

Suddenly, the water was opaque with blood and gore.

<Up! Surface! Now!> I cried.

CHAPTER 8

I dove under a bleeding orca and pushed. Felt another body under mine.

Slowly, up. Up.

<Demorph!> I commanded. <Start now! Everybody. We make smaller targets as humans.>

<Jake . . . I can't . . . >

Who was it who spoke? One or all of us? <You have to. That's an order.>

I clicked and saw the Sea Blade below us. Tumbling. Sinking! Disappearing behind the coral reef.

We had defeated the Sea Blade.

But had I condemned my friends to death in the process?

Had I been so bent on avenging Hahn's death

47

I'd taken foolish risks? Failed to make the right calls? Blundered in like a fool without a clue?

Failed . . .

Frantic thought-speak, all around me. But for some reason I couldn't make out the words.

I tried to say something . . . and couldn't do that, either.

I was losing consciousness. Had I been hit that badly? Had I begun my own demorph?

I clicked and saw — nothing.

Demorph! I told myself. *Demorph!*

Vaguely I felt the changes begin. Or did I?

Vaguely I felt a body beneath mine.

And suddenly, I was being lifted with tremendous force toward the surface. Toward the beautiful night sky. Toward the heavens.

<Jake! My blowhole!>

Too late! I felt my small human body slipping, sliding.

Into the water.

Where I began to drown.

SCHLUUP!

What — !

Suddenly I was imprisoned in a white-ribbed cage!

Water rushed through the bars of the cage and over my drowsy body.

And then — AIR!

Glorious air!

48

The cold, clean air woke me.

Startled me back to bizarre reality.

I lay curled in the massive jaw of an orca. A whale that was breaching, soaring fifteen feet above the surface of the ocean.

And then — "AAAGGGHHH!"

I was flying through that glorious air! Alone! The whale had let me go!

Pah-LOOOSH!

The father of all belly flops!

Wind knocked out of me. Bruised. Disoriented. Gagging on salt water. I thrashed wildly. A spindly human in an endless sea.

There was no choice if I were going to make it.

Brutally conscious, teeth chattering, body aching, I forced myself to morph the orca. A third time.

<Jake? Are you okay?> It was Rachel. <Sorry I had to toss you around like that but you were drowning.>

I clicked. Counted two sperm whales and three orca.

<That's okay. Is . . . is everyone here?> I asked.

<Yeah,> Tobias said. <Our real orca buddy took off a while back. We're here. We're remorphed. And we're ready.>

Marco groaned. <I knew this night wasn't over.>

49

<Rachel? A very sweet save,> I said. <Thanks. We have to make sure the Sea Blade is really out of commission. The last I saw it was still sinking. We locate it, assess the situation, take it from there. Everybody? Dive.>

Again, into the darkness. Beyond the reach of the moonlight. Echolocation our only guide.

<I don't see any sign of it,> Cassie said.

<Maybe it drifted off?> Rachel mused. <I don't know. Is the current this far down strong enough to . . . >

<Look!> I cried. <To the right. About three o'clock.>

It was the Sea Blade. Still listing. Still leaking fuel. Hovering before what seemed to be a cave.

We moved closer. As cautiously as the huge beasts could. Completely conspicuous.

When we were still about a hundred yards away from the ship, we stopped.

<The opening of that cave is far too narrow for the Sea Blade to get through,> Cassie observed. <They can't be hoping to hide, can they?>

<Then what're they doing?> Marco said. <Taking a donut break? If Visser Three was on that sub he'd have bailed. There's got to be an escape sub or something on board, right?>

<One would assume so,> Ax replied. <But none of us has seen another vessel . . . >

50

<Ax-man,> I said suddenly. <Everyone? Straight ahead.>

Through the waving underwater plants that grew around the narrow mouth of the cave came three, four, five — creatures. Vaguely human in shape. Vaguely aquatic.

<Okay, a rescue crew?> Marco wondered.

<From where?> I said.

The five creatures surrounded the Sea Blade. Attached ropes or pulleys of some sort to the ship.

WHHHOOOSSSHHH!

The cave opened wide, simply spread apart.

And then, with an impossibly swift motion, the creatures, whatever they were, drew the Sea Blade through the narrow opening of the sea cave!

CHAPTER 9

<Well, that was weird,> Rachel said.

<Not to mention impossible. How'd they do that?> Marco.

<I think the bigger question is *who* did that?> Tobias said. <They definitely weren't human.>

<Whoever they are, what do they want with the Sea Blade?> Cassie added.

<Prince Jake?> Ax said, questioning, prodding me to decide.

I was feeling like I'd made too many decisions in the last hour or so. Too many bad ones. And yet . . .

<We follow,> I said. <Whatever those were, they could have been some new Yeerk host body

52

or whatever. That may be some kind of Yeerk facility.>

<Yeah, either that or Atlantis,> Marco said with a laugh.

<We're too big in this morph,> Cassie said. <We might get in, but maneuvering inside a cave as an orca? Could end up being sardines.>

<Suggestions, Cassie?>

<Not the dolphin. Nothing that breathes air. Not in a cave. I think we need the hammerheads. Their electromagnetic capabilities might prove useful in an underground environment.>

<Okay. Everybody to the surface and demorph.>

We did.

Four human kids, a hawk, and an Andalite.

I looked at us, bobbing in the midnight ocean.

My best friend. My cousin. My girlfriend.

A *nothlit* and an alien.

My friends.

Bedraggled. Wet. Cold. Incredibly tired.

Hair plastered to their heads. Lips blue. Bodies shivering.

And I was asking them to do it again. Again!

For the third or fourth time in less than an hour.

To morph and dive deep, deep into the chilling dark ocean. To hunt down the Sea Blade.

Sometimes I hate my life.

53

"Let's go, boys and girls."

Again my body shot out behind me. Sleekened. My legs melted together into a V-shaped tail. An elegant dorsal fin rose from my back.

My skin became tough, rough. Sandpapery.

My face . . . my face was not pretty.

It flattened. Widened as rows and rows of teeth marched back toward my throat.

My forehead spread to either side to form two tough fleshy wings.

POP! POP!

An eye appeared at the end of each wing.

My head measured over two feet across!

I could sense food. Prey.

I wanted to kill it. Eat it.

Not bother to swallow it first. Not consider what was sliding down my throat. Not care if it was another hammerhead . . .

<Jake!> Tobias ordered. <Get a grip!>

The human part of me shuddered. I'd grazed Tobias with my teeth. A thin red line appeared on his eleven-foot-long body.

<Sorry, man. I must be tired. Let's go.>

We dove back down to the sea cave. There was no trace of the Sea Blade.

For one small moment I hesitated. And then I thought of Hahn. Anger's a pretty good motivator.

Pride's a pretty good motivator, too. I was going to win this battle. The Yeerks weren't going to

54

escape. Get them now and we wouldn't have to come back.

I had all kinds of good reasons to go forward. No reason for turning back, except fear. And another feeling, like fear, but subtly different.

That cave, those creatures, something about it all gave me the unholy creeps.

<Here we go,> I said.

I led the way through the narrow passageway. Inside the cave, through the giant undulating fronds of ocean plants that obscured, then revealed the opening.

Darkness. Total and complete.

Do you know what that means? Total and complete darkness?

It's a darkness almost unimaginable to a bunch of kids used to seeing the night sky illuminated by neon and streetlights and stars.

It's a darkness that swallows you. A darkness that makes you wonder if you're even alive. A darkness that deprives you of sight and — once you get over the freakiness of being totally and completely blind — makes all your other senses somehow more acute.

<Whew! What is that — smell? Taste?> Marco said.

<Fuel?>

<Great. We're following the equivalent of a fleet of Greyhound buses down here.>

55

<At least it means we're on the right trail,> I said. <The fuel's got to be from the Sea Blade.>

<Probably not fuel,> Ax said. <This is not a human submarine. It is very unlikely to be powered by the incomplete combustion of the liquid remnant of decayed vegetation. That smell/taste is most likely coolant.>

<Ah.>

<Or possibly the waste from the onboard sanitary facilities.>

<I vote for coolant,> Marco said.

The tubular passageway seemed to be about nine feet in diameter. Tight. Too tight for the Sea Blade to have come through. But then the cave seemed to be adjustable.

BONK!

<Uh, guys,> I said. <We've got a dead end.>

No more tunnel. Just a wall of rock.

And five other hammerhead sharks coming to an abrupt, bumping halt in the dark.

<Great,> Marco said brightly. <Okay. Party's over. Closing time. Everybody out. Just turn right around and . . . >

<Marco?>

<Yeah, I know, Rachel. "Shut up.">

<Jake?>

<We're going through that wall,> I said. <Just don't ask me how.>

CHAPTER 10

<Now — any suggestions?> I asked.
BBBBBZZZZZZZZZZZZ!

<Yaaahh!> Marco cried. <What is that!>

<I would venture to say there is an electrical field behind this wall,> Ax said.

<Ugh. It feels like biting tinfoil with a mouth full of fillings!>

<Rachel? How would you know what that feels like?> Marco said. <I always assumed you were a perfect specimen of oral hygiene.>

<Never mind,> she snapped. <What do we do now?>

I moved forward and nudged the wall with my nose.

57

<That, I guess.>

Amazing.

A thin horizontal line of light appeared in the center of the wall. In that profound gloom the light was almost blinding.

<Ooookay. We are so not in Kansas anymore,> Marco said.

The line grew to a rectangle. Then to a square. About four feet by four feet.

And then the square rounded to form a perfect circle.

Brighter greenish squiggles of light pushed out from the flat surface of the circle and formed rotating coils.

<Psychedelic,> Tobias muttered.

<I do not recognize this technology,> Ax observed. <Not Andalite. Not Yeerk.>

<Not human,> I said. <What next?>

Suddenly the coils of green light began to migrate toward the center of the circular panel. When they'd gathered in a bunch, they split.

Opened like a mouth to reveal a tunnel beyond the wall.

<Amazing,> Cassie said.

<Disturbing,> Marco added.

<Single file,> I said. <On me.>

We swam through the opening in the wall. The mouth shut behind us. Sealed up as if it had never been there.

<Well, that's not comforting,> Marco said.

The water on the other side was marginally brighter. At least there was enough light for me to make out a right and left bank of muddy land along the "river" of water.

I surfaced cautiously. And yes, there was a surface.

<I'm going to demorph. See if this air is actually air.>

I demorphed. The air was cool and humid but definitely breathable. The others joined me. We scrambled onto the puddled left bank of the watery passage.

After a minute my human eyes began to adjust to the twilight atmosphere. There was a sense of impossible vastness about this space. Far larger than the Yeerk pool complex. Huge. Endless. A cavern that could have contained Manhattan.

I blinked and squinted. The light, such as it was, didn't seem to have a source. No sun, no stars, no lamps, or stadium lights. It was more like a watery background glow.

I could barely make out the faces of my friends at first. But then my eyes adjusted. They looked tired, scared, but definitely not beaten.

I looked around and saw images appear, slowly becoming visible as my eyes adjusted. But what I saw was impossible.

59

A few dozen yards away was a ship. A wooden ship. It had three tall masts. A single deck of gunports, eighteen in all, all open, all revealing the blunt snouts of old brass or iron cannon. The sails hung limp from most of the yards. The ropes and cables sagged. But nothing was as rotted as it should be. After all, no ship of this type had sailed in almost two hundred years.

It rested in dry dock, on a massive cradle made of carved coral.

"Coral?" Cassie said. "There's no coral near here."

Marco gave her a look. "*That's* what bothers you? The *coral?* There's a whole three-masted frigate sitting there like it just floated in from the War of 1812."

<And a crew,> Tobias said.

"Say what?"

<My night vision's not great, but I see men in the shrouds. And up on the yards.>

"What do you mean, men?" I snapped.

<I mean men. Dead men. Not moving. Not breathing. Just frozen in place.>

"Okay, we're leaving," Marco said.

"Weird," Rachel said.

"Weird?!" Marco shrilled. "Weird?! There's a whole ship with a bunch of dead guys getting ready to raise sail and sing, 'yo ho, yo ho, a pi-

60

rate's life for me,' in an underwater cave the size of Lake Erie, and your feeling is that's weird?"

"Look down there," Rachel said, pointing downstream, past the frigate.

Another shadow loomed. We walked toward it, under the lee of the frigate, oppressed by the sense of those tall masts and the shadowed, unseen dead who tended them.

We moved on toward a ship different yet similar to the first. This, too, was a sailing ship. But older. It was rounder, the masts shorter. There was a sort of ornate castle built up on the stern.

<Spanish galleon?> Tobias speculated.

Here, too, the ropes were slack, the sails hung like sheets on a clothesline on a dead calm day. And here, too, Tobias reported on bearded faces, empty eyes.

"Look, I don't know about anyone else, but I believe in listening to my instincts. And my instincts are saying, 'You've done enough, Marco. Go home. Play with the stupid poodle. Do some homework.'"

"I get the same feeling, Marco," I said. "But we almost got killed trying to take out the Sea Blade. I don't want a rematch. I want it sunk. I want to know it's sunk."

<And this is certainly a fascinating phenomenon,> Ax added.

61

We walked past the galleon. And yet another ship waited for us. Smaller, sleeker.

<PT boat,> Tobias said.

And on we walked, feet thick with mud, hearts beating in slow, leaden rhythm.

"That's not a ship, that's a wall or something," Rachel said.

"It curves outward toward the top," Cassie pointed out. "But it's too big to be a ship, isn't it?"

"Tobias?" I said.

He flapped up and kept flapping. Out of my sight. I waited anxiously. Then he swooped back into view and settled on Rachel's outstretched arm.

<It's an aircraft carrier. It's an *entire* aircraft carrier. Japanese. There's a Japanese flag. That is an entire, World War Two, Japanese aircraft carrier. Impossible!>

"They'd have flares. We could use some light. Also weapons," I said. "Might be worth taking a look. Is there an easy way up?"

<Around the far side. There's an actual staircase. Weirdly proportioned steps, but definitely steps.>

"Let's go."

We crossed beneath the overhang of the bow, as tall as an office building. And there, as Tobias had said, was a staircase.

62

"Think we need to buy a ticket?" Cassie wondered idly.

I led the way up the steps. It was a long climb. But then, at last, I stepped out onto the flight deck of an aircraft carrier. Two Japanese planes waited. Looking like they could take off for Pearl Harbor at any second.

The pilots grinned.

Dead.

The flight deck was as long as a football field. Almost as wide. I led the way to the superstructure. I didn't want to see what was inside. I felt vulnerable in human morph, but we were all exhausted from multiple morphing. And we had Ax. The reassuring, delicate clop clop clop of his hooves was loud in the dense silence. And though he was probably as exhausted as us, his tail could handle most threats.

I opened an oval hatchway. Swung it outward. Jumped back.

There were lights on inside!

"Ax? Up front."

I felt cowardly putting Ax forward, but he did have four eyes. He could see in all directions and react faster than I could.

He stepped gingerly through. <It appears deserted.>

I followed him. Down a narrow hallway. Pipes clustered thickly on the ceiling and occasionally plunged down the walls. The floor was steel, the walls steel.

Ax pushed open a second hatch and stopped. He said nothing. Just stared with all four eyes.

I leaned over him.

It was a fairly large room. At one end a low, raised platform. A map was on the wall. A chart of some sort.

Facing the platform were seats, like the seats of an old theater. Several rows. Perhaps two dozen seats in all. And in each seat, facing forward, dead men.

CHAPTER 11

"They're dead," I said unnecessarily.

"Are you sure?" Rachel said in an oddly small, thin voice.

<They'd have to be. How could they . . . > Tobias's logic trailed off.

<If you like, I will examine the bodies, Prince Jake.>

"Good idea," I said. "You do that, Ax."

"Ax is the man," Marco mumbled.

His hooves ka-klunking on the painted metal deck, tail blade angled forward, poised for attack, Ax stepped through the narrow doorway.

Cassie went with him. I guess this was a medical situation, to her.

Ax leaned one of the bodies forward gently,

65

respectfully. Cassie looked at what he was showing her and gasped.

The two of them came back.

<They are dead humans,> Ax stated. <They have been preserved. Stuffed with a substance I cannot identify without further, more detailed examination, and sewn up the back with a stringy vegetative material.>

"I am so out of here," Marco said. "Jake, we have to go. Now."

"Marco? Shut up," Rachel said, but more like she was trying to quiet her own fears.

"Mummies? Like, what? Like Egyptian mummies?" I asked, feeling stupid.

"Sewn up the back," Marco muttered. "Who cares what style? Dead is dead."

"The bodies are in remarkable condition," Cassie said, sounding like she was talking from some other place, not connected to her own body.

<I am unable to identify the culture or people responsible for this, Prince Jake. This is so irrational and strange that I assume it must involve humans.>

Two dozen Japanese pilots gazed sightlessly at a briefing map. Ready for the attack. Where? Pearl Harbor? Midway? Some forgotten battle?

They'd been the enemy then. Didn't look or feel like the enemy now.

66

"Let's get out of here. Back out on deck."

I felt marginally better outside.

SCREEEEECCCHHH!

Instinctively, I ducked.

A seagull! The bird swooped only inches above our heads and landed on the metal railing bordering the deck.

"Look at the eyes on that thing!"

The creature I thought was a seagull was not a normal seagull.

Its eyes were enormous. They covered the entire sides of its head and touched over its beak. And unlike a normal seagull's eyes, this bird's eyes were bright blue.

<Eyes adapted to a perpetually dim environment?> Tobias guessed.

As if in response the bird squawked, spread its wings, and took off.

"Are we certain the Sea Blade came through this Museum of Lunacy?" Marco said. "Cause I, for one, am all for bailing."

I frowned. "No, we're not sure. But we have to assume it did. And our mission's still the same."

"Destroy the Sea Blade before Visser Three finds the Pemalite ship," Rachel said.

"And avenge Hahn's death," Cassie added softly.

"Let's go airborne," I said. "It's probably safer

67

and we can cover more ground. Tobias, stay hawk. Everyone else, go owl."

Owl. A morph I hoped would allow us to see more clearly in the dim light.

To explore silently.

To defend ourselves if we had to against mutant seagulls and whatever other odd creatures we might find.

Whatever other *live* odd creatures.

A few minutes and we were off again. We followed the river further into this macabre underwater world.

Hundreds of ships for countless square miles! German U-boats. A 1930s vintage tramp steamer. Pieces of junked motorboats. A Polynesian raft.

Rows of periscopes. Broken hulls. Propellers. Ships' wheels. Rudders and radar equipment. Deck furniture from luxury ocean liners.

And bodies.

Preserved pilots and passengers. Eighteenth-century European crew and twentieth-century tourists. Whalers. Fishermen.

<It looks like a collection,> Cassie said. <Almost orderly. Deliberate.>

<Yeah. Mr. Psycho's Nautical Toy Box and Graveyard," Marco added grimly.

<Or a sicko director's movie set,> Rachel

68

said. <Is anyone else expecting to run across, say, the *Titanic*?>

<These ships and boats are from everywhere,> Marco pointed out. <Atlantic, Pacific. Thousands of miles away. That galley has to be from the Mediterranean. This is impossible.>

With my keen owl's eyes I detected a slight glow a few hundred yards ahead. As we got closer to the light I saw that it was coming from the far end of a narrow tunnel.

A tunnel into which the nautical graveyard and the river was rapidly narrowing.

<What now, Jake?> Rachel asked.

I hesitated again. But only for a moment.

To go on was to lead my team — my friends — further into the unknown. And from what we'd just seen on the Japanese carrier, there was a good chance the unknown was seriously weird.

And probably very dangerous.

Or go back. Turn around.

Forget the search for the Sea Blade. Leave it to chance whether Visser Three ever found the Pemalite ship. Stole its secrets. Used those secrets to further the Yeerk invasion of Earth.

The visser. The Abomination responsible for the sickening recent torture and murders of Hahn and forty-nine other innocent Hork-Bajir.

<Keep going,> I said.

69

Twenty-five feet from the light. Fifteen. Ten.
<What the — !>
<Whoa!>
WHHHOOOSSSHHH!
Sucked through to the other side!

CHAPTER 12

<**H**AAHHH!>

Tumbling through the air, feet over head, flapping frantically to regain control!

Five owls and one hawk slapping each other with wings, scratching each other with outstretched talons, awkwardly bumping and twirling.

<AAAHHH!>

I righted myself. Blinked.

<Whoa. Everybody okay?>

<That was kinda fun.> Marco.

<Right,> Cassie said. <Like being caught in a clothes dryer. Or a tornado.>

<Yeah, we're fine, Jake,> Rachel answered.

<Okay. What fresh hell is this?> Tobias said dryly.

71

It took me a minute to focus. To see the differences between this place and the hideous ship museum we'd just left.

It was a city. Sort of. A series of interlocked buildings. Like one of those ancient Indian cliff dwellings made of adobe. Only this city was made from various parts of ships and boats. Massive prows jutted out, tankers, battleships, passenger ships, sailboats. Lifeboats were hoisted up the sides of ships to become terraces. Ships' propellers turned slowly, drawing air into monstrous steel fortresses.

The entire back half of an oil tanker had been planted vertically, so that the ship appeared to have sunk bow downward in the ground. There were gun barrels welded together to form pipes leading from this bizarre water tower into the city.

Several dozen World War I and II vintage submarines were stacked three high. The conning towers and sterns had been sliced off and now revealed only oversized doorways. Maybe they were some sort of storage. A warehouse made of dead subs.

From the center of the city rose a fantastic tower. It was a visual trip through the history of technology. At its base it was constructed of massive iron cannon, welded and bolted upright deck upon deck, rising perhaps thirty feet. All of it was covered in hammered gold and silver, a billion-dollar skin. After that the building materials began to change. Heavy iron plate. Smoke stacks. Massive guns. Steel pipe. Another twenty or thirty feet. And then lighter construction: aluminum sheathing, wire, computer consoles, the tubes of burned out missiles.

The city hummed with the sound of engines. Dim lights burned, here and there. And the air smelled of oil and smog.

<Just when we thought things couldn't get any weirder,> Rachel muttered.

<This is amazing,> Marco said.

<It's like a set for that movie, *The Island of Lost Children,*> Cassie said. <Or like — *Peter Pan* or something.>

<Yeah,> Marco said. <You know, I thought I was joking when I said we might find Atlantis.>

<Kind of skanky for Atlantis.>

<Prince Jake? Ahead. On that — corner. Creatures. Beings. Not,> he hastened to add, <any species with which I am familiar.>

<The people who stole the Sea Blade,> I said.

They were approximately human in size and shape. Two adults and one child. Wearing loose, simple garments. Kind of old-fashioned for Earth. Like togas. Like something the ancient Romans wore. And . . .

<Their skin is blue — not that we haven't

73

seen that before,> Rachel said, glancing at Ax. <Kind of cool, actually,> she added. <But I have to give a "thumbs-down" to the oily look.>

<Jake?> It was Cassie. <Look at their necks. They're . . . they're gilled.>

<And webbed,> I said grimly. <Feet and hands.>

<And the eyes. They're oversized, like the ones on the seagull,> Tobias noted.

<Not a bad body on that one,> Marco said.

That earned him stares from all of us.

<What? What? I can't compliment a fish girl?>

<We come here chasing Yeerks and we end up with this?> Cassie wondered. <Is this good luck or bad luck?>

<It's *our* luck,> Rachel said dryly.

<Let's take a closer look,> I said. <I don't think the Sea Blade is ever leaving here. But let's be sure. And let's be careful.>

I opened my wings and flew, silent as only an owl is silent. My owl's eyes easily pierced the murk and gloom. It was noon on a sunny day to me.

Over the city walls. I had to force myself to focus. This was a find beyond imagining. A city, a species, all right here on earth. Here for a long time, judging by the collection of ships.

It was beyond belief. And yet real.

74

And dangerous, I reminded myself. These people, whoever they were, had stuffed and preserved Viking and Roman warriors, pirates and Royal Navy officers, Japanese carrier pilots and U.S. Marines.

Maybe all those bodies had been dead, drowned before these creatures got hold of them.

And maybe not.

We swept across the city, silent visitors from another world. A squadron of terrestrial predators.

The city was alive and active. There were men and women — if those terms applied — walking along narrow streets. There were workers trundling wheelbarrows or driving forklifts.

There was building going on. I had to look away from the painful blaze of arc welders.

The "river" flowed by the city, then turned and flowed right beneath the walls, through the city, bisecting the weird jumble into two unequal halves.

And there, in the middle of the town, tied up at a dock, was the latest ship to be brought here.

The Sea Blade.

<Let's land,> I said.

<There's a good perch over there, on the tower,> Tobias said. <Looks like a wooden mast. And a crow's nest.>

75

<Well, look what we have here,> Marco said. <The visser's new toy, tied up and ready to be stripped for parts.>

Just beside the Sea Blade stood a bulky pyramid-shaped structure, towering over every other structure in view.

Steam belched randomly from hundreds of turbines that somehow had been attached to small shelves of stone. Shelves that formed a sort of natural staircase to the flattened top of the structure.

<Uh, geography isn't my best subject,> Marco said. <History, either, for that matter. But is anyone thinking what I'm thinking? Aztec? Mayan? Inca? General South or Central American primitive style pyramid?>

<Except for the metal chimneys, yeah,> I replied.

<Because you two guys are experts on pyramids,> Rachel sniped.

I focused on the dock.

<Hork-Bajir,> I said. <Look.>

Emerging from the Sea Blade was a line of seven-foot-tall Hork-Bajir. Twenty-five or so. Being herded along by about ten of the blue, gilled creatures wielding a motley collection of primitive spears and new, automatic weapons.

Hork-Bajir. The visser's crew. Manacled to

76

each other, ankle to ankle, shuffling along, heads bowed. Hands tied in front. Being led into the base of the stone pyramid structure.

<No Visser Three?> Tobias said.

<Not that I can see,> I answered grimly. <He may not have been aboard.>

<Or maybe he's already a prisoner,> Cassie suggested.

<Maybe he escaped capture,> Rachel countered. <Morphed to something small and slipped past the B.G.'s. We've done it often enough.>

<B.G.'s?> Ax wondered.

<Blue Gills. B.G.'s.>

<Weren't they a group, like a long time ago?> Tobias asked.

<Prince Jake? There are only twenty of your minutes remaining in this morph.>

It didn't take long to size up the situation. The Sea Blade had been captured. Its crew taken prisoner. Visser Three. . . . Well, it didn't look good for him, either.

No doubt the Sea Blade and its crew would become the latest exhibit in the gallery of ships.

And when the visser was captured, he'd become the city's most popular circus act. Night after night, until his traveling supply of Kandrona ran out, forced to morph, demorph, and remorph to crowds of hooting gilled creatures.

77

Maybe. I could dream, anyway.

Not my problem. The Sea Blade was down. Gone. Maybe Visser Three, too.

This was a victory. A major one, no less because it was handed to us by the B.G.'s.

Time to be thankful and to get out fast.

<Okay. We've seen enough. We're out of here. Let's find someplace to demorph then remorph. Then we go home.>

CHAPTER 13

We flew away from the city toward an open expanse empty of buildings — and, hopefully, of the blue, gilled creatures.

The light grew dimmer away from the heart of the city. I could more clearly see the dome of the vast cavern. Pinpoints of what had to be artificial light dotted the "sky" but became duller the further we flew. Wide streaks of charcoal-colored cloud obscured many of these "stars."

We flew away from the busy streets of the city until we reached miles of fields. Rubbery tangled vines of green, yellow, and aquamarine covered the ground like a thick, dense blanket of writhing snakes.

79

<What is that crap? Rubber snakes?> Marco commented nervously.

<It does look kind of — alive, doesn't it?> Cassie said.

We landed several feet apart. All except Tobias, who remained airborne as our lookout.

My talons gripped the slimy stems and my wings remained slightly flared for balance. The stems bobbed with the weight of the owl's body but held.

<I believe these plants are growing in water,> Ax said.

<Kind of like water lilies? Their pads can hold the weight of big fat frogs,> Cassie said.

<See?> Rachel said. <Nothing to be afraid of. Just plants. Bizarre plants, but . . . >

<Just demorph everyone.>

Within minutes we were four kids and an Andalite. Balanced precariously — especially Ax — on the shifting floor of seaweed. About to morph again to owls and join Tobias above. About to fly out of this place, this hidden nightmare.

<Jake! Watch out!>

"What the . . . !"

A heavy weight like a prickly blanket was thrown on my head and shoulders and back. I fell to my knees. My body rocked and bobbed as if I'd been tossed on a waterbed.

"Jake!" Cassie cried. "What's happening?"

We'd been captured! Netted! The five of us, a tangled mass of arms, legs, hooves, and tail.

"Not good, Jake, my man," Marco mumbled. "Just got a mouthful of seaweed over here."

"Everyone. Stay calm," I ordered.

"Calm?" Rachel hissed. "Battle morphs and we're outta here!"

"No!"

Then I saw our captors. Three, six — ten of the large-eyed, blue, gilled creatures. They pulled the net tight around us, shoving limbs back through the net's open weave. Finally looping the ends of the net together. They worked silently and swiftly.

<Jake!> It was Tobias. <They came up out of the seaweed. I didn't . . . they were so fast . . . I'll follow them and find a way to break you out.>

Stupid of me. I had Tobias watching the skies. But this was a world of water.

Now they began hauling us across the vines, bouncing, sinking into the water, then back up again. I was shoved into Ax, practically in his belly, my arms tangled with his legs.

"Ax, answer Tobias," I ordered in a whisper. "Tell him it's okay. Tell him to stay out of sight. And to be careful."

Ax transmitted my message via thought-speak.

WHUUUMMPPF!

Tossed almost upside down!

81

"Ow," Cassie muttered. "Ow, ow, ow."

"Jake, this is insane!" Marco said. "Rachel's right. Let's bust out of here. Now! No way these guys are going to be able to haul a bag of gorilla and grizzly!"

WHUUUMMPPF! WHUUUMMPPF! WHUU-UMMPPF!

"We don't know where the visser is," I said. "Don't know what Hork-Bajir might still be loose. We don't even know if these guys might be infested," I said in between getting mouthfuls of dank water.

My knees were crammed into my chest and my left arm was already going numb. But as uncomfortable as I was — as we all were — I knew we just couldn't risk morphing. Not out in the open, in full view, with the visser on the loose.

<I would be happy to sever the net with my tail blade and free us, Prince Jake,> Ax said tightly. <You and the others would not have to morph.>

"No. Not yet anyway. We don't want a fight with these guys. They're civilians, as far as we know. We don't know what we're up against. We wait. Watch."

"I hope you're right about this, Big Guy," Marco muttered.

WHUUUMMPPF! WHUUUMMPPF! WHUU-UMMPPF!

So did I.

CHAPTER 14

Across the field of bobbing seaweed. Back into the heart of the city. Across the splintery wooden dock. To the large doorway at the base of the pyramid structure.

Dragged like a sack of potatoes. Or garbage. We were bruised. Battered. Cut.

Afraid.

Yanked across the threshold. Then pulled across a cold, slimy stone floor.

The passageway was dark.

From somewhere in the distance I heard a shrill cry.

The voice was Hork-Bajir. In pain.

"Is that . . . "

"Yeah," I whispered.

83

I was now pretty sure I'd made the wrong decision.

They hauled us to the center of a large room. WHUUUMMPPF!

And unceremoniously dumped us out of the net.

There was no chance to prepare for who or what we might meet. The room was dim. Lit by the same strange, pinpoint light source we'd seen first in the gallery of ships.

But the room wasn't so dim that I couldn't see a throne against the far wall.

"Real velvet?" Rachel whispered. "I'm impressed."

The cushions were purple. The throne itself was gold, encrusted with pearls and colorful shells. Or pretty good imitations of the real things.

And on the throne sat another of the blue, gilled creatures.

A woman. Dressed in a loose gown woven, I guessed, from some sort of plant. It had a rubbery look not unlike the vegetation we'd just been dragged across. Around her neck were draped ropes and ropes of pearls.

"So do we kneel or bow or scrape our foreheads on the floor?" Marco muttered. "I mean this is some kind of a queen, right?"

Ax stepped forward, tail blade partially raised. At the ready but respectful.

On either side of the woman stood a line of ten guards. Blue, gilled men armed with an assorted collection of spears and handguns. One carried a bow and arrow. Another carried a .50-caliber machine gun with an ammo belt draped over his shoulder. Another a mace, at least I think that's what they were called, a club with an iron head studded with spikes. One had a matched set of beautiful, ornate dueling pistols.

The woman squinted her huge, tennis-ball-sized eyes.

Think of an orange cut in quarters. Each eyelid was the size of one of those quarters.

Then she cocked her head and spoke.

"Ni hau."

"That's Chinese," Cassie whispered. "But I don't know how to answer."

The woman spoke again. *"Hvordan har De det?"*

"Scandinavian?" Rachel wondered. "I wish she'd try a Latin-based language. I wouldn't be able to answer, but I could at least try and fake it."

The woman shifted impatiently on her cushioned seat.

"Guten tag. Wei geht es Ihnen?" she demanded.

"Okay, that's German," Marco said under his breath. "We're getting closer. Some similarities to Eng —"

85

"Bonjour!" she cried.

"Uh, bonjour, madame," I blurted. *"Parlez-vous l'anglais?"*

"Of course," she replied arrogantly. "Since the latter half of the twentieth century English has been considered the international language of commerce and intellectual discourse on the Surface. As Surface-Dwellers you must know this."

In a day full of weird, this was one of the weirder moments. She was a blue-skinned, gilled woman with webbed feet and eyes the size of Whoppers, and she was lecturing me in flawless English.

"Attitude?" Marco muttered. "From a queen? Now there's a surprise."

"I am indeed the queen of the Nartec," the woman declared, rising from the throne. "My name is Queen Soco. And my hearing is quite acute."

"My . . . my friend means you no disrespect, Queen Soco," I said quickly. Placatingly. Remembering the shackled Hork-Bajir. The cry of the Hork-Bajir. The mummified crews and passengers. The Japanese flyers sitting there in a mockery of a briefing.

"Good. Because it is usual for visitors to our kingdom — I am assuming you are not trespassers here to do us violence? — to behave with the proper decorum."

"Yes, Queen Soco. We are visitors from the,

86

uh, Surface. We, uh, we come in peace," I said. Feeling like I was Captain Picard in some old episode of *Trek*. Acting all calm and polite and respectful on the outside, while inside I was tense and alert — and afraid.

"You are the leader," Queen Soco stated. "You speak for the others. Good."

SLAAAP! SLAAAP!

With wide, webbed hands, she clapped twice.

"I require that you be my guests this evening at a traditional Nartec feast," she went on. "I want to know how you came to the land of the Nartec. And I am extremely curious as to the four-legged blue creature that seems to accompany you as a pet."

Ax stiffened.

"The creature is quite magnificent."

Ax relaxed. About an inch.

Queen Soco gestured to the door behind us. An armed male Nartec came forward and stood beside us.

"In the meantime, Naca will be happy to escort you on a tour of my palace. Within these walls you will see many wonders of the Nartec civilization."

"Thank you, your highness," I said.

Marco raised his eyebrows at me.

What else was I supposed to say? What was I supposed to do? I was stalling. Waiting.

87

The guard called Naca gestured for us to precede him to the door. I turned to go — and was stopped by Queen Soco's loud and final words.

"Do not attempt to escape, Surface-Dwellers. That is not a suggestion. It is an order."

CHAPTER 15

We sat around a large round, massively constructed table made of salt-weathered beams. No doubt cut from one of the more badly destroyed wrecks the Nartec Searchers had found and hauled back to their bizarre city. It might be a hundred years old. Or twice that old.

Our chairs were constructed of odd pieces of lumber. Cobbled together timber. A few sported patches of cracked leather on the seats and seatbacks. One was decorated with an inlaid pattern of cracked and dirty mother-of-pearl.

Those sitting nearest the queen, at the head of the table, sat in a bizarre collection of deck chairs and captain's chairs.

89

Plates heaped with raw fish sat before us on the table. Some of the fish were whole. Eels. Small sharks. Octopus. Others were cut up into chunks, kind of like sushi. A few stainless steel bowls, no doubt some fairly recent salvage, were filled with seaweed. Each of us had a mug of — something green.

Marco held up his mug for me to see. His still had a shadow of a logo emblazoned on it. Russian letters and the outline of a nuclear sub.

We were unwilling guests at this traditional Nartec feast. I mean, how comfortable can you feel when you're making a command appearance — and doing it under the watchful eyes of at least fifty armed guards standing at attention all around the room.

Trapped. We couldn't run and we couldn't morph. Not while the Nartec watched.

Not while Visser Three was possibly still on the loose.

He could be anywhere. In this very room. Morphed to some tiny watchful creature. Waiting to make his own escape.

Wondering what humans were doing in the world of the Nartec.

Putting two and two together. Remembering the whales that had damaged his precious Sea Blade.

Realizing the "Andalite bandits" were not Andalites after all.

Stupid! I should have thought of it, should have realized that morphing and fighting our way out of the nets was the lesser of two dangers. Had I been drawn here by my own curiosity? Had I fallen prey to my own fascination with this impossible place?

Should have fought our way out. If a few Nartec were hurt . . .

Should, should, should. I hate the word.

I glanced at Rachel. Her lips were set in a thin line.

Cassie's eyes were wary.

Marco grimaced at the pile of fish in front of him.

And where was Tobias!

Captured? Held in another part of the palace?

Would we suddenly hear the tortured screech of a red-tailed hawk, as we'd heard the screams of Hork-Bajir?

Queen Soco took a sip from her cup and then fixed us with her wide round eyes.

"Now that you have seen the wonders of my palace, I am sure you have many questions to ask. What would you like to know about the Nartec, Surface-Dwellers?"

<Perhaps you should ask her to explain the

91

origin of her people, Prince Jake,> Ax said privately. <The story might provide valuable information that will help us understand our present situation. And make possible our escape.>

It was a good idea. And about the only one we had.

I asked.

She folded her arms over her chest. Closed her eyes and kept them shut for a long minute while I sweated and wondered if I'd committed some offense.

Then she opened her eyes again, but kept her gaze elevated. It was a ritual, I realized, seeing the respectful reactions of the other Nartec.

"This is the story our people have told since the Beginning. This is the Sacred Truth, told again and again, down through the ages. The Sacred Truth of the Kings and Queens of the Nartec."

I had the feeling Marco was suppressing a desire to make some sarcastic remark. I shot him a hard look. He contented himself with only rolling his eyes ever so slightly.

"Many thousands of years ago, the Nartec lived on an island in the middle of the Great Ocean," Queen Soco intoned. "Very slowly, subtly, over time, the island began to sink. Each generation built higher and higher walls around the island to keep the Great Ocean from swallowing the people. With each passing year the walls be-

92

came higher, higher — hundreds of feet tall. Marvels of engineering!"

The Nartec nodded in agreement. A silent chorus playing its part.

"Still, it was inevitable that the pressure of the Great Ocean would cause these protective walls to wear and to bend. Closer and closer they grew until the top of each wall met the top of another and formed a ceiling to our world.

"Then the Great Ocean closed over the Nartec. The island continued to sink. Perhaps it is still sinking."

Queen Soco paused to eat a small hunk of white fish.

<A strange and improbable tale of origin, Prince Jake,> Ax commented. <Obviously it has become distorted over the years of telling until now it is more myth or legend than truth.>

I nodded to Ax, and Queen Soco went on.

"What is important is that the Nartec did not die," she said. "We adapted to our new underground, underwater world. Over time we discovered alternative sources of light. Like that produced by the narna rocks that blanket our roofs and ceilings.

"And, of necessity, our bodies changed, too. At an impressively rapid rate. We became amphibious by an act of supreme will."

Ax commented privately. <Even without the

93

necessary experimentation, I am fairly certain the light produced by the "narna" rocks Queen Soco mentioned is radioactive. No doubt this radioactivity hastened the rate of the Nartec's mutation.>

I nodded again slightly to show Ax I'd heard.

"Thus did we come to build this magnificent city. Thus did we survive and prosper. And thus did we come to be the rightful rulers of the One Ocean and all lands touching her."

The crowd nodded and seemed satisfied. They sat back, relaxed and began to eat again.

Queen Soco took another drink from her cup and continued. Her voice was less formal now. She met my gaze.

"Of course the Nartec continue to study the technology of sunken oceangoing vessels constructed by the Surface-Dwellers. We study construction techniques and food storage methods. We learn of navigational equipment and other electronic devices that might be of use to us. From the large oceangoing pleasure boats we learn about the changing styles of Surface clothing and furnishings and recreational activities. And if there are survivors of the wrecks that bring these vessels to us, we study them, too. That is, until we have learned all we need to know from them."

"Here it comes," Marco mumbled.

"And then?" I asked. Though I knew the answer.

Queen Soco smiled faintly, amused. "Then they are preserved to become part of our storehouse of knowledge."

"You kill them and stuff them," Rachel said.

"Exactly."

CHAPTER 16

"Yeah, stuff this?" Marco muttered under his breath.

I shot everyone a look. *Stay calm,* it said. Like that was possible.

Ask another question, Jake. Get all the information you can. Maybe it will —

"AAAAGGHHH!"

Cassie flinched. Rachel started to rise from her chair but a look from Marco made her sit back down.

Ignore the wail of another Hork-Bajir from somewhere in the bowels of the building. Stay focused, Jake.

Where was Tobias?

"Queen Soco, what are your plans for the Sea

96

Blade?" I asked congenially. While digging my nails into the old, soft wood of my chair.

"In the past," she said, sitting back in her chair, "the Nartec have sent Searchers to the Surface of the Great Ocean. They have traveled in vessels built with the technology and materials made available to us by the salvaged vessels of the Surface-Dwellers.

"However, none have ever returned. It is assumed none survived the journey to the World of Sun.

"You must understand that this is not the fault of the Nartec Searchers. Rather, it is an indication of how the technologies of the Surface-Dwellers are terribly flawed."

Queen Soco sipped from her cup and then continued.

"But with the Sea Blade! It is clear to us that a more intelligent, advanced people than mere Surface-Dwellers built such a magnificent vessel!"

<Yeerks! We Andalites could easily build a ship to put the Sea Blade to shame,> Ax said tightly.

"Our plans are these," Queen Soco continued. "We will send a carefully selected and trained crew of Searchers to the Surface in this powerful new vessel. We will take whatever oceangoing vessels we encounter. We will mount raids on the

97

Cultures of the Sun! We will conquer villages, towns, cities — even larger land masses! We will show all Surface-Dwellers how powerful and advanced are the Nartec!

"The long centuries of our exile are over!"

Several Nartec became so excited they began slapping the table. All nodded and smiled.

I kicked Marco under the table. He shut his mouth.

"That is a noble purpose," I said politely. Quickly. "I have one more question, Queen Soco. It's about the crew of the Sea Blade . . . "

Now Marco kicked me under the table.

<Prince Jake, I do not think it wise to interfere . . . >

I faked a small cough. "Excuse me. I was just wondering what . . . "

"No more questions, I think," Queen Soco said abruptly.

She smiled and gestured with a webbed hand. A female Nartec promptly removed Soco's empty cup and plate. "Now I have a question for you, Surface-Dwellers," she said. "Where is *your* ship? I know you did not arrive in the magnificent black vessel. I know the Sea Blade does not belong to you."

I had no answer. I shot a glance at Ax. His face was unreadable.

"I see." Queen Soco rose from her chair. The

meal was over. "Perhaps you need some time to create a plausible lie. Or to come to your senses."

Halfway to the door Queen Soco turned to face us. We were still sitting motionless at the table.

"I will discover the truth, Surface-Dwellers. Have no doubt of that. But I am also a magnanimous queen. Feel free to further explore the Nartec world. We will meet again later." And then she grinned. "Perhaps."

The door closed behind her.

I smiled awkwardly at the remaining Nartec, then led the way out of the room. We paused in a small chamber adjoining the main hall.

"We are so out of here!" Marco grabbed my arm. "There is no reason — NO REASON — for us to hang around. Do you hear me Jake!"

I shook off Marco's hand. "I hear you. And if you don't lower your voice, the entire Nartec people will hear you, too. Ax? Cassie?"

"I'm with Marco," Cassie whispered.

"I'm *not* happy about bailing without having found the visser," I said grimly. "Or destroying the Sea Blade. Queen Psycho may have delusions, but she could still do a lot of damage with the Sea Blade."

<The Yeerk vessel could sink any human vessel,> Ax agreed. <It could also carry out Dracon

99

attacks on Earth's coastal cities. However, eventually human defenses would be able to crush it by sheer weight of numbers.>

"Cool. So we leave it to the navy, and we book out of this nightmare," Marco said. But then I saw his eyes cloud. He looked disturbed.

"What?" I asked him.

"I was holding a mug from an old Soviet nuclear sub. They may have more than Dracon beams to play with."

"You don't think the missiles survived?" Cassie demanded. "Aren't they protected with all kinds of computer codes and so on?"

Marco nodded. "Yeah. Absolutely. And the Nartec probably can't beat the security measures."

<Probability is not certainty,> Ax said grimly.

"Great. So Queen Psycho maybe has nukes. Wonderful."

"And what about Tobias?" Rachel demanded. "We're going to leave without him?"

I shook my head. "No."

"That's your decision? We stay?" Marco asked.

"I could put it to a vote," I said with a smile for my old friend.

Marco shook his head. "I'll follow you, Big Guy."

"Okay. Look, we have the run of the place. So,

100

A) we find Tobias, B) we destroy the Sea Blade. And C — "

"C — we haul our soggy butts out of here and forget this lunatic asylum even exists?" Marco interrupted.

"Got that right," I said.

CHAPTER 17

"What's your take, Ax?"

Ax looked up from the pile of books and ledgers on the scarred wooden table in front of him.

We'd continued our tour in the palace's library. If you asked me, the most interesting room in the palace.

I don't think of myself as narrow-minded. But I was still waiting to discover one of the "wonders" of Nartec civilization.

Human mummies — especially those made from the bodies of prisoners and slaves — are not my idea of high culture.

Neither are hidden torture chambers or room

after room of scavenged, mostly decrepit stuff, randomly piled and stacked.

But the library. A place filled floor to ceiling with shelves. Those shelves lined with documents made of some vegetable material. Pounded. Woven, maybe, into sheets of "paper."

Pages bound together by some tough and stringy substance. Marked with what Marco jokingly guessed to be the ink of giant squid.

Who knew? Maybe he was right.

In addition though to these mostly indecipherable Nartec scrolls were thousands of water-stained human books in every imaginable human language: ships' logs, novels, lists, atlases, maps, and charts. Everything that might have sunk with a ship or been thrown over the side in centuries.

Naca, our own private watchdog, escorted us to the large room and stood at attention just inside the door.

We weren't trusted not to attempt to escape. But we had been trusted with the Nartec's plan to conquer Earth with the Sea Blade. And now we were trusted with the Nartec's entire written history.

What did information matter to prisoners who were going to die before they could tell tales?

But the flip side of the coin was: Why waste time? Why not kill us right away? Why make nice?

103

<Prince Jake, assuming the basis of Queen Soco's story is true and the Nartec originated on the Surface — that is, on planet Earth — and given the Nartec's apparently accelerated rate of adaptation to this underwater environment — an acceleration confirmed here in these ancient but remarkably well-preserved and annually updated population records . . . >

"Like births, deaths, plagues, natural disasters?" Cassie asked.

<Yes,> Ax confirmed. <As well as a detailed running account of each Nartec generation's physiological and biological evolution — or devolution — from a land-dwelling mammal to a completely amphibious creature.>

"Devolution?" Rachel glanced over her shoulder and gave Naca a falsely bright smile. "What do you mean by that?" she asked tensely, turning back.

<It is my assumption — and you must remember that without proper experimentation and my own documentation . . . >

"Ax."

<Yes, well.> Ax straightened his shoulders in a way that made it clear dealing with lowly humans was a sacrifice for a lofty Andalite.

Especially an Andalite who'd been referred to as a pet.

<I believe the Nartec are self-destructing.

They are profoundly inbred. As I believe humans know, insufficient variety in the gene pool can lead to deterioration over time. The Nartec population is dropping. Fertility is dropping. Infant mortality from birth defects is rising. Life spans are shorter.>

"You mean they're on the brink of extinction?" Cassie whispered.

<Yes. The high levels of radioactivity have allowed them to undergo accelerated rates of mutation. But now the destructive mutations are beginning to pile up. And they have insufficient sources of new genetic material.>

"Why?" I asked.

Cassie had the answer. "Fewer ships sinking. They must have been breeding with limited numbers of surface humans, survivors of sinking ships."

Ax nodded. <It would be at best a short-term and dangerous fix. The new breeding stock would no doubt have resulted in a relatively large number of Nartec born without their unique adaptations: gills and webbed feet.>

"So their dreams of conquering Earth are —"

<The desperate act of a race that knows itself to be doomed.>

"How horrible," Cassie said. "An entire people — gone."

"Oh, yeah, I'm weeping over here." Marco

snorted. "These people are planning to mummify us. After killing us. And if those Hork-Bajir screams are any indication, after *torturing* us. As far as I'm concerned," Marco added, "the Nartec can just devolve to extinction right now."

Cassie coughed and looked embarrassed. "Actually, Marco, they may try to breed with us first. Or at least extract our DNA, if that's possible with their technology."

"Marco may finally get a girlfriend," Rachel said with a laugh. "Of course she'll have gills . . ."

I grimaced. "Look, we've got an immediate threat here. The Nartec have captured the Sea Blade. We can't let them take it to the surface."

"Which means?"

"Which means," I went on, gently closing one of the old books on the table, "that we have to either destroy the Sea Blade right where it is or steal it from the Nartec. Use it to get out. Then destroy it."

"How are we going to destroy it at the dock?" Marco hissed. "It's sitting right out in the open. Right in front of a palace filled with armed soldiers."

Rachel said, "We slip away from this Naca guy — knock him out first if we have to — morph and . . . "

"And what?" Cassie shook her head. "What's a grizzly going to do to a ship the size of the Sea

Blade? Even if we sink it the Nartec could probably raise it and repair it. These are people who manage to drag entire supertankers across two oceans."

"Cassie's right," I said. "Our only choice is to steal the visser's ship. Get it away from the Nartec. Destroy it later using the ship's own weapons."

<Prince Jake, I wonder if I might mention a possibility we have not discussed?>

I nodded.

"Why do I know this is something I don't want to hear?" Marco said.

<Has it occurred to you that Visser Three, using his many morphs, might still be aboard the Sea Blade?>

I nodded. "Oh, yeah, Ax. It's occurred to me."

107

CHAPTER 18

"This area surrounding the palace is inhabited by those Nartec of better families," Naca said solemnly. "Those of great wealth and prestige."

Naca stood erect, carrying what I believed to be a German, World War II vintage submachine gun, and pointed toward the artificially lit "roof" of the Nartec world. Incongruously, there was a sword in the scabbard at his waist.

Two other Nartec guards had joined us when we'd left the palace. They flanked our little group. Silent. Keeping a particular watch on Ax. Their odd collection of scavenged weapons at the ready.

Marco sidled up beside me and drew me back, out of earshot of Naca.

"We can take these guys, Jake," he said.

"Maybe," I said.

"They've got it coming. Is that what's bothering you? If you're worried about hurting some, hey, these people are evil squared. They could go one on one with the Yeerks in the Evilpalooza."

I shook my head and smiled at Naca. "We've tried dozens of times to take down Visser Three," I said. "Always failed. He's hard to beat. Hard to get to. You think these guys did it? I don't. I think he's here."

"We don't even know for sure he was on the Sea Blade. He may —"

"He was on it," I said. "He doesn't delegate glory to his subordinates. If he found the Pemalite ship he'd be the man again. For the Yeerk hierarchy, the Council, all would be forgiven. He's here."

Marco shrugged. "Okay. He's here. Let's leave him here and get out."

Naca was moving us along, and looking suspiciously at me and Marco. "If we can get out of here, so can he, Marco. The Sea Blade is going to be dust, Marco. Vapor. Visser Three isn't going to have it, and neither is Queen Soco."

We were walking along again, tourists in the land of the weird. With a blue tuna-man for a guide.

"The Nartec who specialize in law, medi-

109

cine, and other such professions," Naca continued, "dwell in the area just outside the central part of the city. Those Nartec employed in the trades — such as those who make our clothes and sell our food — occupy a more remote neighborhood."

With a disdainful flip of his webbed hand, Naca gestured to the distance.

"Finally, those who scrape together a living in an obscure or illegal manner inhabit dirty, shanty-like towns on the outskirts of the Nartec world. There is no point in my taking you to see such places. They are unpleasant and not at all important."

"Nice to know discrimination is alive and well among the Nartec," Cassie mumbled. "I feel so . . . at home."

I listened vaguely to Naca's tour guide routine. Pretended to be really interested in a small building decorated with a carved and painted wooden prow. The kind shaped like the body of a woman with arms held tightly to her sides and legs that kind of disappeared somewhere.

And now that I was paying attention, a woman wearing not a lot of clothes, either.

"Any apartments for rent in this building?" Marco asked.

Slowly, steadily, we were moving away from the dock, away from the center of town.

Every move seemed natural. Too natural. Too casual. Every move too smooth. Too practiced.

I had the sudden conviction that Naca had done this before. Many times. I wondered how old he was. How could I tell with one of these creatures?

Old enough to have been alive in World War II? Had he led the Japanese flyers on this same path?

If only we had Tobias. I missed my eyes in the sky. My air force.

We were approaching a building built out of the center portion of a white-painted ship. Bow and stern were gone. The superstructure was intact. A sort of baroque office building perched at the top of steel cliffs.

There was a faint outline in red. The outline of a cross.

"This was a hospital ship," Cassie said.

"Yes," Naca agreed. He nodded like he was pleased. "I would like to show you our medical facilities."

We were on a causeway over a canal. The causeway was narrow, built of the gray, steel catwalk of some ship.

No signal had been given, but I was sure the trailing guards were moving closer. Sure that fingers were closer to triggers. Hands tighter on the hafts of spears.

111

"Not necessary," I said tightly. "I'm sure it's a great hospital."

"But it is a great scientific treasure of our people," Naca insisted. "Queen Soco would be mortally offended if —"

"I don't like hospitals," I said.

No illusion: The guards were moving closer. But they could only get two abreast onto the causeway. Ax had drifted back to bring up the rear. Ax would take down both guards before they thought about squeezing a trigger.

I shook my head, feeling fairly secure. "I don't think so, Naca."

What happened next happened so fast I had time for only one thought, one last stab of regret.

Amphibians, Jake. Amphibians.

With a rush the hidden Nartec shot up out of the water on both sides of the causeway.

CHAPTER 19

I woke up, eyes open suddenly.

I tried to move. Couldn't. I was strapped down on a table. Facedown.

Shot a look left, right, Cassie on a table beside me. Stainless steel operating tables. Beyond her I caught a glimpse of Rachel, likewise strapped down. Marco? I couldn't see him, but he could be next to Rachel.

Ax?

I twisted my head as far as I could.

"Do not squirm or resist, it will accomplish nothing," Naca said. "Soon you will be injected with a concentrated liquid from the *ablata* weed. It will render you peaceful and compliant."

113

His bug-eyed face loomed over me. Two new Nartec faces as well.

"And then what?" I asked.

"And then we will make an incision from the top of your skull, down to your buttocks, then down along the back of each leg. Your ribs will be removed, then your internal organs, and eventually the rest of your tissue."

"What are you doing this for?" I demanded, a little frantically.

"Your organs and tissue will be processed to extract the helical molecule that controls heredity and later employed to augment the development of —"

"There are easier way to get new DNA, you idiot!" Marco yelled.

Naca continued unperturbed. "Then, your skin and bones will be stuffed and preserved to be used in our educational facility."

"Okay," Rachel said. "Jake? Now can we kick these guys' butts for them?"

The answer was yes. But I couldn't say it. Couldn't say it because something had happened to my mouth. My lips were rubber. My face was frozen. My hands were tingling.

The injection!

I couldn't move. Couldn't . . . but it really didn't matter. What was I getting so tense about? No need to get all worked up.

"Jake . . . I . . ." Rachel said. Then, slowly, from far away . . . "Never mind."

I knew what was happening. I knew we were being drugged. Knew it meant death. Knew it meant me and my friends being eviscerated, stuffed . . .

Couldn't manage to hold on to the outrage.

Couldn't . . . focus.

All lost. Didn't matter.

Faces swimming above me, around me. Huge eyes. Blue skin. Knives in their hands. Cold steel on my neck . . .

A new face. New Nartec. Carrying a mace, an ancient, medieval club. Like Sir Fishalot.

Hah-hah-hah . . . what?

He looked at me.

Then he slammed the butt of the mace into Naca's ribs. Naca went down, sinking with magical slowness past my face.

A dreamy, upward swing caught the next Nartec on the chin. The third one turned and ran.

I heard a door slam. Heard a wheel spin.

Then the mace-wielding Nartec was back. He was back, but not the same, anymore. His rubbery, blue skin was now covered in a spreading pattern that looked a lot like feathers.

115

CHAPTER 20

It took several minutes for my head to clear. By then Tobias had morphed back to the red-tailed hawk.

There was loud banging on the door of the operating room.

"Tobias? Nice to see you, man."

Rachel gave him a hug — or as close as she could come with a bird. Then she yelled at him, "Cut it kind of close, didn't you?"

<Hey, you try finding your way around this nuthouse. Those Nartec morphs are weak, slow, and easily tired out of the water. They're much stronger in the wet. But probably not ten percent of the population is strong enough dry to go on a long walk. This Naca guy is one of the lucky few.

116

Like the guards they let you see. My morph was not so good.>

I nodded toward the closed and locked steel hatch. "Bad guys out there?"

<Yep. Lots of them. One by one they aren't too tough, but fifty of them, armed, is another thing.>

"Now about Ax?"

<Oh. He's in there.>

He pointed to a second, smaller hatch. Rachel spun the wheel lock and yanked it open. Cold air blew out. It was a refrigerator. An airtight one.

Ax stepped out looking about as mad as I've seen him.

<I suppose my DNA was not good enough to improve this pathetic species,> he said archly.

"Don't complain," Cassie said. "You wouldn't have enjoyed the extraction process."

<I am not afraid of needles.>

"They use the entire body. Grind it up and process it, and stuff whatever is left," Cassie explained.

<Ah. Well, they are merely mutated humans. One can only expect so much.>

"I screwed up," I said. "I forgot they were amphibious. That's how they surprised us on the causeway. But they don't know we can fly." I pointed at the round, open porthole. "They'll get in here soon. Let's be somewhere else."

117

We morphed. The Nartec broke down the door just as the last of us cleared the porthole and took to the air.

<Where to?> Rachel said.

<The Sea Blade. Visser or no visser, I've had it. We're taking that ship and getting out of here. Tobias? Can you get us back?>

<Oh, yeah. I've gotten to know this city pretty well in the past few hours.>

<I'm glad you're okay, Tobias,> Rachel said. <I hate it when you don't get taken prisoner with us.>

<Yeah, well, I was worried about you, too.>

Tobias led us back to the air over the dock. We landed in an alley not much different from the alleys we used at home. Trash is trash, I guess, anywhere in the galaxy. It was the equivalent of two blocks to the Sea Blade.

<Okay. Demorph. Then let's get ready for a fight. We go in hard and fast.>

<You mean Rachel-style?> Marco mocked.

<Yeah. Let's do this Rachel-style.>

Feet and paws and pads pounding, hooves clopping, we ran toward the wooden dock. Through the narrow Nartec streets. Across stretches of sand and mud and shells.

Past staring Nartec citizens. Mothers pulling their kids out of the way. Vendors crying out as we pushed over carts and stands in our path.

A tiger, a bear, a wolf, a gorilla, a hawk, and an Andalite, we managed to be the strangest sight in this, the strangest of places.

<There it is!> Cassie cried.

I heard voices rising. The dim rumble of a crowd forming.

<Prince Jake. I believe word of our escape has reached Queen Soco.>

<Yeah. Tobias! Do you see a way into the ship?>

<It's wide open. A main hatch just behind the raised bump on its back.>

<Show the way.>

Tobias dove for the open door. Slowed so we could see where he went. He was first inside, but Rachel was just a few feet behind. Several Nartec tried to block her path. She hit them like a runaway bus.

Nothing stands where a grizzly bear charges. Nothing made out of flesh and blood, anyway.

We piled through in her wake. She grasped the edge of the heavy, metal door with one massive paw and —

WHAAAMMM!

Threw the door shut and with Marco's help slid the bolts into place and secured the latches.

<Prince Jake.> Ax's voice was grim. <I request some assistance in removing the visser's former crew from their stations.>

119

We hurried on through a corridor that led into a central control room.

And stopped dead in our tracks at the threshold of the bridge.

<Oh, God . . . > Cassie gasped.

Mummified Hork-Bajir.

Sitting upright in the various chairs for pilot and other crew. Standing at a video display screen. Leaning over a radar map.

I swallowed hard to keep the bile from rising in my throat. <Forget them,> I snapped. <Work around them. Push them aside, we have no time.>

Though the mummified Hork-Bajir weighed considerably less than they had alive — with bones and blood and muscle — it still wasn't easy to remove their stiff bladed bodies from the crew's stations.

And it wasn't easy to touch them.

Knowing they'd been breathing only hours before.

Remembering the Hork-Bajir cries I'd heard while in Soco's palace.

Remembering Hahn.

<Ax? Can you operate this thing?>

Ax stood at the main control panel on the bridge, his back to us. <The ship has been adequately repaired. At least as far as I can tell. However, there is a security protocol I must now attempt to bypass.>

120

<Tobias? There's a porthole. What's up outside?>

He fluttered over and looked outside. <Not good, Jake. We've got a crowd gathering. And it's not happy. Maybe a hundred of them out there. Armed.>

I ran over to look out the porthole. It was as he'd reported. A crowd of Nartec armed with spears, rifles, flamethrowers, machine guns, swords, clubs, grenades, and longbows.

The crowd was on the move. Coming for us. <Ax?>

<Nothing, yet,> Ax said, his voice agitated. <The security protocol is far more complex than I had hoped — or assumed. I cannot access the ship's weapons until — >

Buh-Boom!

Sheeeeeeewowww!

WHAMMMM!

The Sea Blade rocked violently in its berth.

<We're under attack!> Rachel cried.

I saw smoke curling from the barrel of a five-inch naval gun mounted atop Queen Soco's palace.

More and larger guns were slowly traversing, bringing their barrels to bear on us.

They couldn't miss at this range. The Sea Blade had been crippled by a pod of killer whales. Those shells, some as heavy as small cars, would blow the Sea Blade apart.

121

CHAPTER 21

<Ax, sooner would be better than later,> I said.

<Or too late,> Tobias said.

Buh-Boom!

The five-inch gun had fired again.

Sheeeeeeeewwwwww!

The shell screamed toward us.

WHAAMMMM!

My tiger paws kept me from falling over from the impact. But Ax sprawled, scrambled back up.

<It blew the outer hatch!>

<Here they come!> Tobias reported from his perch near the porthole.

122

I heard rapid, rushing footsteps on the deck outside.

<How are we going to dive with a blown hatch?> Rachel demanded.

<Ax? Stay on it. Tobias, rear guard. Everyone else, with me!> I ran toward the outer hatch. That was the place to stop them.

I reached the hatch and waited, braced for the onslaught. It was quick in coming. A body of Nartec came swarming. But a swarm can't move through a hatch designed for Hork-Bajir in single file.

A spear lanced by my head, and shredded my left ear. It was followed by the Nartec who had thrown it, wearing at least three other crude weapons on his body.

I backed up, waited till he was framed in the hatchway and leaped. I hit him, paws out but claws retracted. The impact knocked him back into his brother Nartec.

A Nartec warrior nimbly leaped over his fallen friend and I batted him down in mid-leap.

One after the other heavily armed Nartec warriors swarmed toward me.

Old and young. Each one grasping a weapon. Another weapon strapped to his side or back. Some with knives held in their teeth.

Walking arsenals.

123

We were trapped! Nothing to do but to fight!

And now, someone had decided to go to more modern weapons.

BlamBlamBlamBlamBlam!

Twanggg!

The machine-gun bullets ricocheted off steel bulkheads. One passed through my right hind leg. Another through the haunch directly above it.

The pain staggered me. My right rear leg was weakened. I backed up, gave way to Rachel.

She moved with the deceptive grace of the huge grizzly bear and more than filled the opening.

BlamBlamBlamBlam!

Hhhhoooroarrrrr!

An unwary Nartec leaped at Rachel, armed only with a sword. Rachel grabbed him in a bear hug. Literally. One massive arm wrapped around the helplessly struggling mutant. She held him with absolute ease. His weight irrelevant to her power.

And she used him as a shield.

The gunfire stopped instantly. The Nartec saw that they could not fire without killing one of their own.

But they evidently felt safe enough using spears, swords, and other handheld weapons.

Rachel had only one hand free. That was enough for the first dozen or so attackers. But then . . .

"RROOOOAAARRR!"

A harpoon, clear through Rachel's right shoulder!

With a loud grunt she broke off the shaft.

With a ham-sized paw she swatted at the head of a Nartec rising to his feet. He fell back.

But now Rachel gave way, staggered back as the wound took its toll. The Nartec poured into the gap.

Marco punched and pounded. Cassie tore and shredded.

Tobias joined the battle. The Nartec's oversized eyes made clear targets for Tobias's talons.

We were fighting hard and fast.

But still the Nartec flooded the room!

They weren't great warriors. They were physically weak. Some ran away in panic. But they had weapons. And they had courage.

They kept coming, pouring into the dock, pushing through the doorway, filling the corridor . . .

CLAAANG! CLAAANG!

Harpoons bounced harmlessly off the Sea Blade's hull. I glanced up through a porthole to see more Nartec scrambling up the sides of the ship, their webbed hands and feet helping them climb.

125

THWAP! THWAP! THWAP! THWAP!

The Nartec's slapping footsteps on the deck above us.

<Ax!>

<Progress. But not enough to attempt launch.>

We couldn't lose this battle! We couldn't let the Nartec use the Sea Blade. We couldn't let the ship survive.

And we had to get back to the surface!

I bit and tore, leaped and scratched. But we kept backing up. Back to the bridge. Back to where Ax stood working feverishly. In seconds we'd have to pull him into the battle. And then . . .

We were cornered. There were just too many of them! They were exhausting us with sheer numbers.

Blood ran down my haunches from the points of handheld spears.

The harpoon wound in Rachel's shoulder oozed badly.

Cassie was panting, her sides heaving, her right front paw partially gone.

Marco had a short sword protruding from the black, leather chest of his gorilla morph. Shocking to see.

Even Tobias was wearing out from struggling to gain altitude over and over again in the small, relatively low-ceilinged space.

From diving, talons outstretched. Raking one Nartec face after another.

Something had to give.

Something . . .

BOOUUUSSSSHHHH!

CHAPTER 22

BOOUUUSSSSHHHH!

A massive blast of heat and light from the corridor!

Ten, twelve Nartec at the mouth of the hall fell to the floor, their skin smoldering. They crawled away, desperate to escape.

<What the heck was that!> Marco yelled. He held up his right arm. The dark coarse hair was singed from sturdy fist to shoulder.

<The visser!> Ax hissed. His stalk eyes were turned back toward us, his main eyes still glued to the computerized control board.

<How can you tell?> I demanded.

<It is the Luminar. A beast from a moon of

128

the planet Slegabb Five. What else but the visser in morph!>

Into the control room came the Luminar.

A blinding glow!

Blasting heat!

Heat emanating from the very skin of the beast. Seven feet of blowtorch!

Two short arms and two stubby legs protruded from a bulbous body. Sausagelike fingers. A wide smile, crackling with electricity.

A bleeding Nartec scrambled to his webbed feet and tried to scurry past the creature, into the corridor.

The Luminar extended one fat finger toward the Nartec.

SSSSZZZZZ!

Fried! A charred body collapsed in charcoal flakes to the floor.

I felt my stomach heave. The smell was revolting!

<Okay, we didn't need that,> Marco said.

The Luminar pointed again. At each living Nartec still in the control room. Wounded or whole.

And before they could scream or cry or run . . .

SSSSZZZZZ! SSSSZZZZZ! SSSZZZZZ!

Piles and heaps of charcoaled Nartec flesh! Before any of us could — could what? Save the Nartec, our enemy? Absurd. And yet, though we

129

hadn't asked for this battle, though the Nartec were prepared to murder us, though we had all the moral right of self-defense, we had tried to avoid causing casualties.

The visser was simply killing.

The Nartec ran in final panic. And now there was no one in the room but us and the visser.

With a grin that sent tingles like painful static electricity down my spine, Visser Three slammed the inner door shut.

<I hope I haven't broken your concentration, Andalite.>

<Not at all,> Ax replied coolly.

<Good. Then you may fire engines as soon as possible. Oh, that's right.> The visser chuckled. Small licks of flame shot from his mouth. <You can't — unless I help you.>

I swallowed my disgust and spoke to him. <What makes you think you'll be going anywhere with us, Yeerk?>

<Because you need me, fool. Your pathetic morphs were not successful in holding off the Nartec. Clumsy warriors though they are, there are many of them.> The visser chuckled. <And they have many, many weapons. Now that they have failed to retake this vessel, they will destroy it. You may have noticed the large cannon atop the palace. Primitive human weapons, but very effective at this range.>

130

<And why would we trust *you*? Why should we believe you're not going to kill us, too, the minute the ship takes off?>

The visser-in-morph took a step further into the room.

Involuntarily I stepped back from the intense heat flowing from his body. We all did.

<You should trust me because you must. And because I need you to man this ship.> He gestured toward the piles of Hork-Bajir and shrugged. <My crew is — how shall I put this — incapacitated?>

<Jake, don't trust him,> Marco warned privately.

<And what if we say no?> I said. <What if we force you off the ship right now?>

The visser chuckled again. <In that case we all will die. In one unpleasant way or another. You will be fried. Burnt beyond recognition. I will be tortured and mummified or ingloriously murdered by an antique Earth weapon.>

<Prince Jake.> Ax's voice was tense. <I am still unable to breach the security protocol.>

I shot a look at my team.

Rachel growled menacingly but had stepped back to lean against the wall.

Marco was on the floor. The protruding sword still stuck out awkwardly in front of him. The pain must be awful beyond imagining.

131

Cassie held her front right paw off the ground, her body trembling.

Tobias favored his left wing.

This was insane! An impossible situation!

Maybe. Maybe not.

<Everyone,> I said privately. <I'm going to ask the visser to turn off the security protocol.>

<Yes, Prince Jake.>

<Jake, are you nuts?> Rachel hissed.

<Sometimes,> I said. <Let's hope now isn't one of those times. Timing is everything. Be ready. Be very ready. The moment will come.>

I turned to face Visser Three.

<We accept your . . . offer.>

CHAPTER 23

<What was that you said, Andalite? I must not have heard properly.>

<You heard me,> I said. Struggling to maintain control. <We accept.>

The visser's Luminar mouth split into its bright, crackling grin. Small plumes of smoke shot from its nostrils. <As I knew you would. One can always count on two things from Andalites: That they will adopt a sanctimonious moral posture. And that when it serves their purpose, they will quickly abandon that posture.>

Ax stepped nimbly away from the main station. The visser took his place and the Sea Blade shivered and hummed as the engines came to life.

<There are more coming!> Tobias said from his perch at one of the portholes. <And a group of Nartec are running back along the river.>

<Keep watching, Tobias,> I ordered.

<You may pilot the ship, Andalite,> the visser said now, allowing Ax to resume the pilot's position. <And one of you may take the weapons station.>

<Rachel,> I said.

<Um, Jake? I don't know how to run one of these — >

<Ax will tell you in private thought-speak,> I said. <Just play the part.>

Ax guided the ship away from the dock. Turned it and began to power down river.

<Marco? Can you close the outer hatch and hold it?>

<Maybe. Not when we get out into the ocean, though, dude. The water pressure . . . >

<I don't think the visser knows the hatch is blown,> I said. <He didn't come from outside. He was aboard the whole time. If you can do it . . . >

<What, this little sword in my stomach? I can do it.>

Marco lumbered away.

<Where is he going?> The visser demanded.

<To remove the sword from his stomach,> I

said calmly. <He would prefer not to scream in pain in the presence of a Yeerk visser.>

<How are we going to get through to the museum cave?> Cassie asked me.

<Ax, take her down, just enough to submerge us.>

<The hatch.>

<Ax. Just do it, please. And then, as we approach the barrier, instruct Rachel in blowing it open.>

All that was in private thought-speak. In the open I said, <Fire when ready!>

<I give the commands on this ship!> the visser roared.

<Not to my people,> I shot back.

TSEEEWWW! TSEEEWWW!

The high-powered Dracon beams tore through the wall of rock surrounding the narrow tunnel.

<Cassie, Tobias. Keep an eye on the visser. And watch the exterior screens.>

<Oh, yeah.>

We powered along the river, just below the surface. Exterior cameras showed us the Nartec's macabre collection of seagoing vessels and peoples. A graveyard of Earth's cultures.

A history lesson I would have preferred to have missed.

A history lesson I would never forget.

135

We were alone in a Yeerk ship with Visser Three.

<Jake!> It was Cassie. <They're coming after us!>

<German U-boat,> Tobias added.

<Andalite! Fire!> the visser roared.

Ax said rapidly, <Rachel, you can target the pursuing ship's rudder without damaging the ship itself,> He gave her instructions. Rachel stabbed at the controls with her Trent Reznor nails.

<On my commnad,> Ax said calmly. He put the Sea Blade into a sudden starboard turn. The U-boat was at an angle to us, baring her stern.

TSEEEEEW!

We fired. The U-boat stopped, dead in the water.

The visser sneered. <Pity for the weak. An admirable character trait. It was Andalite pity that allowed us to emerge and begin the conquest of the galaxy.>

<Wall ahead,> Cassie reported.

TSEEEEWWW!

We blasted our way through the second rock wall.

Zoomed along the narrow pitch-black river, the sides of the massive ship scraping and gouging the muddy walls of the tunnel.

<One more,> I said privately. <And then, everyone be ready.>

Then in open thought-speak, <Prepare to fire. Fire!>

136

TSEEEWWW!

<Keep it up,> I ordered.

The beam burned through the water, sliced through living rock. Turned water to explosions of steam.

<Prince Jake. There are several mechanically propelled, cylindrical objects coming at us from behind. They appear to be propelled by primitive electric engines turning small propellers.>

<Torpedoes!> the visser cried, seeing the display. <Three minutes to impact. We can easily outrun them. Maximum power, Andalite! We'll be in the open sea within seconds.>

<NO!> Private thought-speak.

<Jake! You okay man?> Tobias said.

<I'm fine, buddy. Ax. Kill the engines. Marco? Open the hatch.>

<Oh, man,> Rachel moaned.

The engines suddenly quieted.

The visser turned violently away from the control board. <You betray me?!> he roared. <I will incinerate you!>

Just then the wave of seawater exploded through the doorway and flooded across the bridge deck. The visser's burning feet were suddenly mere flesh.

<Interesting morph, Visser,> I said. <Does it work underwater?>

137

CHAPTER 24

Water rushed into the room, an out-of-control surge of green seawater.

<Rachel! Grab Tobias!>

Tobias was in the most danger. Birds don't do well in the water. Rachel wrapped him in her powerful embrace, and the water swept over us.

I was swept into a bulkhead by the force of the water. Slammed, but softly.

Saw Cassie already upright and swimming through the water toward the outer hatch.

Saw the visser, demorphing as fast as he could.

Saw Ax seeming to walk through the water, his four hooves galloping almost comically.

Rachel powered by on main force.

The water stung my eyes. Filled my nostrils.

138

Deafened me, annihilated my sense of smell. The tiger did not panic — it was one cat that could swim — but I was scared just the same.

The surge of water relented once the bridge was filled with water. I could swim. But could I breathe?

How long till the torpedoes hit?

And how much damage would —

B-B-BOOOOMMMM!

B-B-BOOOOMMMM!

One, two torpedoes. Exploded!

The Sea Blade rocked. My eardrums were blown in by the concussion. I lost my sense of direction. Floated, lost, confused, into a half demorphed Visser Three. Pushed away.

The Sea Blade rolled sluggishly. Sinking!

Yes, bow down. I was sure. My tiger senses were not evolved for this, but still the tiger knew up from down. The Sea Blade was sinking.

SHSHSHWUUUUPPPP!

Suddenly I was out. Out of the ship. It fell away from me, two broken halves. Then the stern half snapped in half again.

I swam like mad, straight up. Up to the air!

My orange-and-black-and-white head burst through the barrier between water and air. I was still in Nartec territory. Still in the river that wound through the hideous Nartec museum.

I could see the looming bulk of the Japanese

139

aircraft carrier. Those flyers had been my country's enemies. Now friends.

My mind flooded with that awful image: the men, the warriors, turned into stuffed, mounted displays.

I submerged and began to demorph.

As a hammerhead shark I swam through the falling rocks, the wreckage we'd made of the Nartec's defensive wall.

I found the others in similar morphs out in the clean, open sea. A gathering of sharks. And one orca, Cassie.

<Everyone here?> I asked.

<Yeah, we were just waiting on you,> Marco said.

>The visser?> I asked.

<I just echolocated,> Cassie said. <I saw what looked a bit like a giant squid. Leaving the vicinity of the cave entrance.>

<Heading which way?>

<Toward land,> Cassie said. <Toward land.>

The visser had survived.

But so had we. Barely. My own mistakes would keep me awake at night for a while to come. But I'd been in charge for a while, now. I'd gotten past thinking I would always be right.

It's a war, I reminded myself. *You did what you could, Jake. You tried to do what's right. You tried not to make it any worse than it had to be.*

140

And you got everyone home alive.

We headed back toward shore, away from the nightmare world beneath the sea. Back toward our own gentler civilization.

<Filthy creatures,> Rachel spat. <Someone needs to wipe them out.>

<The Nartec?> Cassie asked.

<Who else? What they did to all those people? All those sailors? Those flyers back there? Filthy, sick creatures. As bad as the Yeerks.>

<I believe you overlook one fact,> Ax said.

<Yeah?>

<All those sailors back there, all those humans the Nartec . . . defiled? Many of them have sunk in storms or hurricanes, or by the failure of primitive human technology. Many. But not all.>

<So?>

I knew where Ax was going. I said, <So the rest? Including those Japanese flyers? They were sunk. By humans, in human wars. Not by the Nartec. The weapons they used on us? Human weapons. We want to hate them for what they do? Maybe we should stop helping them do it.>

Rachel was silent for a while, then she said, <Okay, fair enough. But you know what? We win this war someday, get rid of the Yeerks, and everything comes out and all? We need to go back, show people what's down there, get busy.>

141

<Start a whole new war?> Cassie asked.

<No. Not to fight,> Rachel said softly. <To bury.>

<Amen to that.>

I said, <Let's get out of here.>

Don't miss

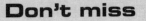

#37 The Weakness

WHOOOOOOOSSH!

I climbed to my feet.

Tried to leap after it.

Where was it? There!

Only air!

THUUMPF!

I fell again.

WHOOOOOOOSSSH!

<I can't even see it!> Cassie cried.

ZZIIIIISSSSPPP!

<See what?> Marco. <A-uumpfh!>

In seconds — if that — it had us herded into a trembling, panting, tangled cluster. Four incredibly fast, incredibly agile hunters, subdued.

The thing made me think of pulled taffy.

Or of a cartoon depiction of speed.

You know, where the cartoon character's skin stretches as he strides faster and faster — until his skeleton runs right out of its skin suit.

That's where this thing belonged. In a cartoon. Where the impossible is possible.

An impression. A flash. A blur.

A small whirlwind or tornado.

And then it stopped. Suddenly.

Came to a dead clean halt. No slowing down. Just — stopped.

<What the . . .>

It was a creature. Now I could see that clearly. Not a machine but flesh and blood.

A bizarre creature able to zip across the grass like a high-speed insect.

Like a bullet fired from a thirty-thirty. A hunting rifle.

Only about as tall as a gazelle.

Four lanky, skinny legs. A thin but strong-looking tail, as long as its body, that flicked and twitched even when the creature's legs weren't moving.

A pigeon chest, high and rounded.

A head shaped like a custom-made aeorodynamic bike racing helmet. Tight curved face, like half a smooth ball. Skull that swept back from the rim of this ball into a pointy triangle. Like an ice cream cone on its side. Except the cone was flattened.

But what really caught and held my attention was the fact that this thing was covered in blue fur.

And had no mouth.

And sported two thin, weak-looking arms.

Like an Andalite. Like Ax.

<Bail! Just go!> Tobias called frantically. <I'll distract it.>

But Tobias didn't have to distract it. The creature suddenly left us — and appeared at the bedraggled visser's side. In the time it took to blink.

<Now!> I cried.

We ran, fear and the dregs of adrenaline helping the exhausted cheetahs to relative safety, scattered throughout the thick woods surrounding the valley.

We got away only because the creature had let us. I knew that.

And I didn't like it one bit. It made me angry. More annoying, it made me nervous.

Why had it let us get away?

We demorphed, on our way to our usual bird morphs for the trip home.

And we listened to the creature speak with Visser Three.

Thought-speak. Superfast.

The words became clear a beat after the creature had stopped speaking. A time delay between sound and meaning.

Kind of like when you talk on the phone to someone in Europe. Or any other continent, I guess.

<Apatheticdisplay, VisserThree.Youarechased downonaplanetyoushouldlongagohaveconquered. Thiswillgoinmynotesyoucanbesure.>

<You too failed to capture the Andalite bandits, Inspector,> the visser sneered. Loudly.

<Depriveyouofwhatisyourdutyandresponsibility?Andmyenjoymentinwatchingyoufail?Finally, youwilladdressmeasCouncilorThirteen,Visser.>

<You're not a member of the council, yet. Not until you have received final approval,> the visser stated flatly.

The inspector made a sound that could have been a laugh. High and trilling. A sound that sent chills up my temporarily human spine.

<Ihavebeengivenaspecimenofournewestand mostcapablehostspecies.TheGaratron.Iwillnotfail tobepromoted.>

Kneeling on the dark soil, my back bent, hair hanging down over my face, a twig imbedding itself into the skin of my right palm. A human palm.

Still feeling, strangely, some of the cheetah's exhaustion.

But it was too dangerous to delay. I took a deep breath and rushed right into the next morph.

In what seemed like seconds, I had brown-and-white feathers, massive wings, a hard, cruel beak.

I was a bald eagle.

<Everyone?> I called privately. <Take off, one at a time. I'll go last. Tobias first, Ax, Marco, and Cassie. Meet back at the barn.>

<Rachel?> It was Tobias. <I'll wait for you.>

An Incredible Discovery Has Been Made...

ANIMORPHS

K. A. Applegate

The place where Visser Three feeds has been located. The Animorphs agree that the time to confront their greatest enemy is now. The mission calls for top speed and agility. After acquiring cheetah morphs, the team is ready for the chase.

There is a problem, though. While Jake's away, there is no one assigned to lead the Animorphs. Which Animorph will rise to the challenge? And will the new leader be able to take on the unexpected dangers that arise?

ANIMORPHS #37: THE WEAKNESS

Watch ANIMORPHS on NICKELODEON TV

Coming in DECEMBER!

Visit the Animorphs online at www.scholastic.com/animorphs

ANIT599

TRANSFORMERS™

ANIMORPHS™

< MAKE THE CHANGE >

Now you can collect your favorite Animorphs characters—
in action figures that change before your eyes!

Hork-Bajir/Visser Three

Tobias/Hawk

Marco/Beetle

Invading Toy Stores Everywhere

Hasbro

SCHOLASTIC

ANIHT499

Step Inside the World of

www.scholastic.com/animorphs
The official website

Up-to-the-minute info on the Animorphs!

Sneak previews of books and TV episodes!

Contests!

Fun downloads and games!

Messages from K.A. Applegate!

See what other fans are saying on the Forum!

It'll change the way you see things.